CONTENTS

MY BiG
Bedtime
STORY BOOK

D. L. : BI-1 400-81

CLIVEDEN PRESS

The Adventure of TWO-TONE

Two-Tone stood alone in his bright red house at the end of Windmill Lane. All was very quiet and had been so for about a week. You see Two-Tone was a little Fire Engine who was stationed in Hollow Bottom Tree Village.

"Oh dear," he said to himself, "I feel so lazy not doing anything!"

If there was a fire, or someone wanted help urgently, he would speed through the village, perhaps showing off a little, calling out "Two-Tone, Two-Tone," as loud as he could, and all the people would stand back and stare, some with interest, others in admiration, as they watched his progress down the road.

Now one afternoon Basil Drake had been invited to tea at Badger Den, the home of old Henry Badger. Also invited for tea were Maurice Mole, Celia Mouse and Gertrude Goose, the tea being held in honour of his worship, the Mayor, Harry Hedgehog.

They all arrived at Badger Den around three o'clock as they were going to have a chat about village

matters, and in particular about Two-Tone. Two-Tone was too noisy and drove too fast through the village, and he did not do all that amount of work anyway. So they decided that Two-Tone could go back to the big City; that would give the villagers a lot more peace and quiet.

Basil Drake was delighted with the decision because, as he

pointed out, the last time Two-Tone came down the road, he was crossing at the corner shop as Two-Tone came round the corner and clipped his tail feathers.

"Most undignified!" he protested, and all Two-Tone did was to hoot and hoot at him, never stopping to say he was sorry or anything.

They all sat down to tea. Iced Buns, pots of honey, and lemonade were plentiful, and the fire burned brightly in the hearth and they all felt snug and comfortable.

All at once there came a rumble from the chimney and soot began to fall onto the fire, filling the room with smoke and dust.

"Oh dear, oh dear," exclaimed Celia Mouse, "I can't see." And all around her they were coughing and choking.

Mr. Badger was grumbling and Basil Drake was quacking his head off, doing nothing but causing utter confusion.

Harry Hedgehog being the leader of the village, in his capacity of Mayor, ran outside to call for Two-Tone.

Suddenly, the bell rang in the Fire Station—"Fire at Badger Den!"

"Whoopee, I'm off!" shouted Two-Tone with glee.

Down the road he went shouting as loud as he could, and going as fast as possible.

When he arrived at Badger Den, Celia Mouse was sitting outside, twiddling her singed whiskers, Badger himself was still grumbling, Hedgehog was scurrying to and fro, not quite knowing what to do but at the same time trying to look important, as if he was in full control of the situation.

Basil Drake was putting out his smouldering tail feathers in Badger's Lily Pond and Gertrude Goose, she was strutting up and down tut-tutting as loud as she could, occasionally stopping to give a hiss of absolute disgust at the whole affair.

Two-Tone soon got to work putting out the fire with water; then he sent for Mr. Dog, who ran the Ambulance, so that First Aid could be given to Celia Mouse's whiskers and Basil Drake's tail feathers.

"Very efficient indeed," said Badger.

"Yes, very efficient indeed," applauded Mr. Hedgehog. "I really think that we shall have to reconsider the position of Two-Tone!" he said, and all the others agreed.

Now if you ever go to Hollow Bottom Tree Village, you can still see the bright red Fire Station, and inside, proudly standing ready for any emergency, is Two-Tone.

Jorinda and Jorindel

In a castle in the middle of a dense wood there lived an ugly old witch. During the day she became an owl, only returning to her own form at night. Anyone who walked too near the castle she changed into a statue or a nightingale.

One day a young shepherd named Jorindel took his sweetheart for a walk in the wood. Too late, Jorindel realised that they were very near the castle, for in the grounds were the statues of youths, once mortal like himself.

Pretty Jorinda did not realise the danger, and went on along a path to pick wild flowers, singing as she went.

Suddenly the singing stopped, and before his dismayed eyes, Jorindel saw the old witch change his dear Jorinda into a nightingale. The witch seized the nightingale and put her into a cage. In vain Jorindel pleaded with the witch to free Jorinda from the enchantment.

She laughed at him and ordered him home, and as he stumbled back through the wood to tend his sheep on the nearby hill the witch mocked him crying:
"In a prison cage I've bound her,
With my magic I'll surround her,
Never more shall she be free,
Hence, young lad, away with thee!"

Jorindel pined for his lost love for many days, and then one night he had a strange dream. In the dream he plucked a purple flower, with a heart of pearl, and using this flower as a talisman he ended the witch's enchantment.

When he awoke Jorindel travelled over hill and dale searching for the flower and at last, at sunset on the tenth day, he found it. As he touched the gates of the castle with the flower, they sprang open and Jorindel entered the castle to the sound of hundreds of birds singing.

He followed the singing until he found the witch, surrounded by seven hundred birds, each in a magic cage. When the witch saw Jorindel she flew into a rage but she could not harm him because he held the magic flower.

Jorindel feared he would never find Jorinda's cage. But then he saw the witch trying to leave the room with a cage in her hand.

"That is my Jorinda!" he cried, seizing the cage and touching it with the magic flower. In an instant his dear love stood before him again, the enchantment at an end, and the witch disappeared in a puff of smoke.

Jorinda and Jorindel used the magic flower to release all the other youths and maidens from the wicked witch's spell, and they returned them all to their families who were overjoyed to see them again.

When Jorinda and Jorindel married, everyone came to wish them well. And as the years passed the sound of children's laughter echoed through the rooms of the witch's castle, and only real nightingales sang in the trees.

Noah's Ark

"You really must go on a diet,"
Brontosauras said to her mate.
"The Ark will be leaving next month
An you're 35 tons overweight.

"You'll never get onto the gangway
It's only fourteen feet by five.
It's too far to swim and if you don't slim
The Brontosauri won't survive."

The Dodo, he flew up to Noah
With a booking form clutched to his beak.
"Sorry," said Noah, "we're full up,
The cabins were taken last week."

The Dodo said "That doesn't matter,
We'll go to Mount Ararat by air."
But they flew far too high, found nothing but sky,
So the Dodo didn't get there.

The dinosaur at the last minute
Rushed home to pack his trunk.
His mate had to wait and she sighed,
"I fear that our future is sunk."

They kept them a place in the queue,
Behind a brown bear and a cow.
The Ark sailed away, they watched in dismay,
And you never see Dinosaurs now.

WIN the lonely GIANT

One warm spring day Win the giant sat outside his cave in the middle of a great forest. His elbows rested on his knees and his chin rested on his hands. He was very miserable.

"If only I could find a friend," he sighed, "someone to talk to, someone to keep me company— anybody at all who wasn't afraid of me."

Sadly he watched the birds flying to and fro with twigs for their nests, and the rabbits basking in the sun. He would have loved to make friends with them, but he was so large and made such a noise when he moved about that all the wild creatures ran away and hid till he had gone.

No other giants lived near and although Win had every comfort a giant could want, he was unhappy.

For a long time he sat there in the sunshine, staring into space; then, suddenly, he had an idea.

Far away, at the edge of the forest, was a village. At one time Win used to walk that way whenever he felt lonely and miserable, hoping that he might be able to make friends with some of the villagers. But they were so afraid that they would run and hide whenever they heard him coming. The small fields, streets, lanes and the village green were always deserted, so Win would walk sadly home again.

"But what would happen," he asked himself, "if they didn't know I was coming?" He began to feel much more cheerful. "If I tiptoed through the forest they wouldn't know I was there, so they wouldn't hide." The idea seemed better and better the more he thought about it. "I may be able to show them I only want to make friends before they run away!"

Win jumped to his feet, not even noticing how the small forest creatures fled from him in fear. He went into his cave, carefully combed his hair and washed his face. Then he put on his hat, his boots and his best jacket and set off.

At first there was no need to walk quietly, but as Win drew near to the edge of the forest he put the first part of his plan into action. He walked on the very tips of his toes, putting his feet down as quietly as he could. He was very careful not to tread on any fallen tree trunks which might splinter and crack noisily.

Soon Win was in sight of the edge of the forest. In the distance he could just see the fields sloping down to the village and the spire of the village church sticking up over the hill. It was time for the second stage of his plan. He took off his strong leather boots, knotted the laces together so that they could hang round his neck, and walked gingerly on in his red-and-white striped stocking feet.

Just before stepping out of the trees and into the fields, Win paused to look round. Many of the villagers were out sowing seed or ploughing, cattle were grazing down by the river, and Win could see children playing on the village green. He was so pleased that he could hardly stand still.

"Oh, I knew it was a good plan!" he said to himself excitedly. "I'll step very quietly into this field, and then I'll begin to talk to the men who are eating their lunch over there, under that tree. I'll have to talk in my kindest, gentlest, quietest voice, but I know they won't run away when they hear what I have to say."

Smiling and full of confidence, Win stepped out of the trees, but unfortunately he forgot to look where he was putting his feet. He took a second step and put his large red-and-white striped stocking foot down right on top of the plough the men had been using before they stopped for lunch. All his thoughts of speaking gently and quietly flew from his mind.

"Ow! Owowowowow!" he bellowed, holding his injured foot in both hands and hopping thunderously on the other, while his boots swung round his neck in a most alarming way. *"Oh Owowow!* Whatever have I stepped on?"

Gradually as he rubbed his foot it began to hurt less and he realised he wasn't seriously wounded after all. He put his foot down and soon he could stand on it without it hurting much at all.

He stood up and looked round, remembering suddenly the reason why he had taken off his boots in the first place.

"Oh no!" he cried. "They've all gone!"

And so they had! There was not one man, woman, child, animal or bird to be seen anywhere.

"After all that!" said Win to himself, very sadly. "I'll never make friends with them now. Bother that plough! Everything was going so well. Just think how I must have frightened everyone! They'll never forget it, never!" Tears came into his eyes. "Well," he said miserably, "I can't do any more harm, I suppose. I'll go and sit down over there where there's plenty of room—and no ploughs—and put my boots on."

Slowly, he tied up the laces, thinking sadly of how lonely he would feel in his empty cave that night, and then, overcome by the misery of it, he cried loudly into his handkerchief.

Then, between sobs, he thought he heard something. He held his breath and listened. From somewhere quite near he heard a little voice say, "Excuse me, but can I help you?"

Win looked all round for the owner of the voice, but he couldn't see anything.

"Where are you?" he asked. "I wouldn't like to sit on you by mistake."

"I'm in this tree," said the voice. "Please, could you lift me down?"

Win parted the branches of the tree and there was a little girl. Her hair was brown and curly with a red ribbon in it, and she wore a blue and white dress.

"Jump off that branch onto my hand," he said, "and I'll sit you on my knee."

Win began to feel more cheerful. He blew his nose then put his handkerchief away. He looked down at the little girl.

"Why aren't you frightened of me like the others?" he asked.

"I was until I heard you crying," she said, "but then I knew that you must be very sad and lonely, so I wasn't afraid of you any more."

"I want to make friends with the people of the village," said Win, beginning to feel sad again, "but I don't know how to begin. I didn't mean to frighten them just now, but I trod on a plough and I didn't have my boots on at the time. I didn't mean to shout like that."

The little girl thought for a minute.

"They think you eat people," she said.

Win interrupted. "But I'm a vegetarian!" he protested. "I eat fruit and cheese and nuts—not people! I only want to make friends!"

"Well," said the little girl, "when they see that you've not eaten me they'll feel much braver. Let's go and look for them."

"What's your name?" asked Win on the way. "You can tell me, now that we're friends."

"It's Julie," she said. "What's yours?"

"if he's so friendly why did he make that dreadful noise? That's no way to treat your friends, making them jump out of their skins very nearly!"

"No, indeed it isn't," agreed the others. "Certainly not!"

"I really am sorry," said Win, "but I couldn't help it. You see, I was walking in my stocking feet so as not to frighten you, when I stepped on a plough. I'll show you the bruise—look!" and he rolled down his sock.

Everyone was impressed and said that they quite understood.

"It's not such a nice name as yours," he answered. "It's Win."

Julie looked up at him. "It suits you," she said.

So Julie and Win went to find the people of the village. Julie told them all about Win, and when they saw that she wasn't afraid they felt rather silly. Some of them even pretended they hadn't been hiding at all.

"Win is very lonely," said Julie, "and he wants to make friends with us. He's not the sort of giant who eats people. He's a vegetarian!" And then she explained what that meant, because hardly anyone knew. "He eats fruit and cheese and nuts—not meat," she said.

"Well," said one of the villagers,

That night Win and the villagers had a great feast. Win carried the wood for the fire, and went to fetch some of his own food for everyone to share. Wherever he went he took Julie with him, perched high up on his shoulder.

"It's fun up here!" she cried. "Now I know what it feels like to be tall like you!"

Win had never been so happy in his life. So many wonderful things were happening all at once. The villagers were having a feast in his honour. He had found many friends, and best of all he had found Julie.

They talked about themselves, told stories, sang, danced and laughed about the things that had happened that day. Win sat at the head of the table as he was the guest of honour, and Julie sat next to him.

"Do you mind having to go home again, all on your own?" she asked.

"Not really," said Win. "When I get lonely I can always come and see you. I could do with some company, but it's not far to the village."

"Ah!" said Julie after a few minutes. "I've had an idea, but I'm not going to tell you what it is!" She smiled mischievously.

Win felt disappointed but he didn't say anything.

Soon the food was eaten, the fire died down and it was time for everyone to go home to bed. Win promised that he would come to the village the next day and help the farmers to plough their fields. He had a large rake which would do the job perfectly. He also promised to help the woodcutters in the forest by pulling up a few

back, and there, curled up snugly inside was a mother cat with five tiny kittens.

"Oh thank you, Julie!" cried Win. "Thank you very much. I shan't feel lonely at home now! I couldn't with this family all around me. Aren't they beautiful!" And he held out the basket so that everyone could have a look. Then he took off his hat, placed the basket in it, and tucked it very carefully under his arm.

"Goodnight, everyone!" he called. "Goodnight, Julie, and thank you! I'll come again tomorrow morning."

He strode off into the dark forest. He thought happily of how well his plan had turned out after all, and of the small family feeling warm and sleepy, safe inside his hat.

trees and carrying them to a place where they could be sawn up.

Happily Win said goodbye to everyone and looked round for Julie, but she was nowhere to be seen. No one could find her.

Then someone cried, "Here she is!" and Julie appeared from the direction of the farm where she lived. She was carrying something in a basket—rather a large basket for her.

"I've brought you a present, Win," she called, and she held out the basket so that Win could pick it up. "Open the lid," she said.

Very carefully Win lifted it

CIRCUS CLOWN

With your great big boots
And the plum on your nose,
You are a funny fellow
From your wiggy to your toes.

You wallow in the custard,
Slither on a pie
And, crashing from the piano-stool,
Heave a big sigh!

You make tea from a kettle-drum,
Toot your saxophone,
And down your baggy yellow pants
Drop an ice-cream cone.

You doff your little bowler,
Squirt water from a rose;
But tell me, are you happier
When everybody goes?

An Elephant for Bindu

It was winter and it was foggy. Bindu didn't mind the snow or the frost. The frost made lacy patterns on her windows and the snow was soft and fun to play in. It floated down like scraps of cotton wool.

But Bindu hated the fog. It was a thick, nasty blanket that choked her.

Bindu caught cold. Her cheeks burned with fever and her throat burnt. Her friend Mary called every day but she wasn't allowed to visit Bindu for two weeks.

"We don't want you ill also," explained Bindu's mother as she thanked Mary for her gift of fruit.

At last Bindu was well enough to have visitors.

Mary crept up the stairs and into Bindu's bedroom.

Bindu was propped up by pillows. She looked tired, and when she coughed her small body shook and her chest hurt. She tried hard to smile at Mary.

Before long the fever had gone and Bindu's cough was no more than a tiny croak. She was al-

23

lowed out of bed. But still she wasn't well. She was cross and grumpy.

"I don't want anything to eat," she grumbled, pushing away the tempting meals her mother cooked for her.

"I don't want to go out," she said sulkily when the fog had all gone and the sun was shining once more.

"Now, young lady, the fresh air will do you good," declared the doctor, scolding her in a kindly way. "You must go out."

"I want an elephant," muttered Bindu, but the doctor didn't understand.

So Bindu went out with her mother and Mary. She wore a warm coat and a fur hood. She shivered and said her legs were cold and tired.

"The child has had a nasty attack of bronchitis," the doctor told Bindu's mother. "It's quite normal for her to feel weak and irritable for a time. What I can't understand is, why she doesn't improve. Children usually bounce back to health very quickly." He frowned thoughtfully. "Let her spend as much time as possible with her friend Mary. I expect she needs young company to cheer her up."

But Mary found Bindu wasn't fun anymore. She was sulky and everything Mary did was wrong. Soon the two friends were quarrelling.

"I hate England," burst out Bindu. "It's cold and wet and nasty and there are no elephants."

Mary didn't know what to do. She told Bindu's mother all about it.

Bindu's mother nodded. "She's talked and talked about elephants to me too. All she says is, 'I want to see an elephant'. I've promised to

24

take her to the Zoo when it is Spring, but she still talks about the elephants.

Mary's mother said Bindu must miss India very much.

"She was very young when we left," Bindu's mother remembered. "We packed all we had into a truck and we travelled a long way overland. Bindu was excited. It was an adventure. But she cried a little at saying goodbye to all her friends. We saw many animals on the journey. We saw a big herd of elephants." She shook her head. "But Bindu cannot miss India. She was so little and she has many friends in England now."

"It was a big, strange thing to travel so far to a new land," said Mary's mother wisely. "Perhaps that is why she remembers the elephants now when she has been ill."

Mary had been listening quietly to all this. If she could find an elephant for Bindu perhaps her friend would be well again. But

the zoo was closed for several weeks yet.

She had a good idea. She found a sheet of paper and a pen. Carefully she sat down to write a letter. It took a long time and sometimes she wasn't sure how to spell the words, but at last she wrote: 'Dear Mr. Zooman, Can you find an Elefant for Bindu as she is not wel and needs one. Pleese help me becos Bindu is my friend. Love Mary.' Then she put the letter in an envelope and addressed it to the zoo.

Two days later a man knocked on Mary's door. Mary's mother was surprised when he said he was from the zoo. He explained about Mary's letter and said he would like to help. Mary's mother

told him about Bindu's illness. Mr. Parker, as the man from the zoo was called, thought it was wonderful of Mary to take so much trouble for a friend. He was sure he could think of something.

Bindu was surprised when a car

arrived to take her and Mary to the zoo.

"But the zoo is closed," said Bindu.

Mr. Parker laughed. "Yes, but the animals still live there." He tucked a warm rug round Bindu's knees. "Come along and I'll introduce you to *my* friends."

Mr. Parker's friends were rather special. There was Willie the chimpanzee, and Zulu the lion. The children laughed and laughed when the Mynah bird greeted them with 'Watcha Pal'. They fed Rolly the pony, and stroked Twitchy the rabbit.

Then at last there was Annie the elephant.

What a moment it was when the keeper led Annie out for a special walk. The children climbed some steps and scrambled onto Annie's tough, broad back. Off they went for a ride. How proud they were.

"Hurrah," shouted Bindu. "It's just like India." And she patted Annie's head. Annie obliged by giving a loud trumpet call, just as if she knew how important a ride it really was.

Mr. Parker smiled. He didn't tell Bindu that Annie was an African Elephant. I don't think Bindu would have minded. She was much too happy.

"Mary, you are the best friend anyone could have," she declared.

"*You* are *my* best friend too," said Mary warmly.

They climbed off Annie's back, down the steps and back to the ground. They stood with glowing faces, hand in hand.

One little Indian girl; one little English girl.

And, of course, one African Elephant.

THE MICE AND THE CAT

There was once a cat who lived in a big house, and he was so keen, and so quick, that the mice of the house lived in constant fear of their lives. One day they decided to hold a meeting to see what could be done, and all the mice, old and young, collected together.

The oldest mouse called them all to order, and one by one they described their terrible experiences with the cat, and gave their suggestions for plans to improve their lot. However not one of the plans was good enough, until a very young mouse stood up.

"I have a plan that can't fail," he told the other mice. "If the cat wore a bell round his neck we would hear it tinkle every time he moved, and so we would know when he was coming, and could run away." The little mouse sat down proudly, well pleased with his plan.

There was a murmur of approval from the other mice, for they too thought it was a good plan. But then the oldest mouse called them to order again. "I agree that it is a good plan," he said, "but who is going to be the one to put the bell around the cat's neck?"

MORAL: IT IS EASIER TO THINK OF A PLAN THAN TO PUT IT INTO ACTION.

Mrs Blue Tit's Springtime Adventure

It was Springtime. The sky was as blue as it could be, with billows of soft white clouds that looked like candy floss, and the sun was warm. It was the time for taking deep breaths and singing loudly for all to hear.

It was a time for being busy too. Jeremiah Jackdaw was busy, very busy indeed. He was helping his wife to build a nest, ready to hold the eggs in about a week's time.

"*Jack jack,*" he sang loudly.

He wasn't a musical bird, and to Mrs Blue Tit sitting close by in the apple tree, the noise was deafening.

"To build, to sing, it's the call of spring," continued Jeremiah loudly.

The noise was too much for Mrs Blue Tit.

"Do hush, Jeremiah," she called crossly. "Anyone would think you were the only bird who could build a nest."

Jeremiah was quite taken back, and rather hurt too. But it was such a lovely day that he couldn't stay hurt for long.

"Whatever is the matter with you, Mrs Blue Tit?" he asked. "You are usually such a happy person."

Which was true. But today even the call of spring wouldn't cheer up Mrs Blue Tit. You see, she couldn't find a nice cosy nesting box anywhere to build her nest in. It certainly was a problem. She told Jeremiah all about it, and

"The one on this tree has coal tits nesting in it," she began, pointing down the trunk where two tiny coal tits could be seen buzzing in and out of a tiny box with twigs and moss in their beaks. "And there are great tits nesting in the one on the almond tree," she continued. "And the nesting box on the plum tree is falling to pieces, and it isn't cosy at all."

Jeremiah felt very sorry for Mrs Blue Tit, but at the same time he felt a little annoyed. If she had started looking earlier she wouldn't have the problem. And it wasn't the day for problems, it was a day for doing things. Then Jeremiah had an idea.

how Mr Blue Tit had been searching for days on the other side of the meadow.

Jeremiah was most sympathetic. "What about looking somewhere nearer home," he suggested.

That was the worst thing he could have said. Mrs Blue Tit was so annoyed she puffed her feathers out till she was like a fluffy yellow and blue ball.

"Why not ask the birds who live in the woods if they know of one," he said to her.

Mrs Blue Tit thought this was a brainwave, and she flew off straight away, nearly forgetting to thank Jeremiah for his help.

Mrs Blue Tit flew into the wood. There were primroses and wood anemones carpeting the

ground, and in tiny sheltered hollows there were patches of deep purple violets.

"If I find a nesting box here," said Mrs Blue Tit, "I can line the inside with primroses and violets and it will smell so sweet for my babies."

Nearby on a tall ash tree she saw Mrs Wood Pigeon. She was enjoying a short rest in the warm sun.

"*Coo-coo-c-cuk*, what can I do for you?" she cooed.

"Do you know of a cosy little nesting box where I could build my nest?" Mrs Blue Tit asked her.

"No, I do not," Mrs Wood Pigeon replied. "I build my nest in a tree, why don't you do the same?"

"It wouldn't be cosy enough for me," replied Mrs Blue Tit. "But thank you all the same."

Mrs Blue Tit flew deeper into the wood until on the branch of an enormous beech tree she saw Mrs Wood Owl fast asleep.

"Come on, come on," interrupted Mrs Wood Owl. "Do tell me what it is you want, then perhaps I can get my sleep."

Mrs Blue Tit took such a large breath that it all came out in a rush. "Do-you-know-of-a-cosy-little - nesting - box - where - I - can build-my-nest?" she asked.

"No, I do not," said Mrs Wood Owl. "I build my nest in a hole in a tree. Why don't you do the same?"

"It would be too dark for me," cried Mrs Blue Tit. And she flew away as fast as her wings would carry her before Mrs Wood Owl had time to reply.

Mrs Blue Tit left the wood and, flying across the meadow, she met Mrs Cuckoo.

"*Cuckoo, cuckoo, cuckoo*," called Mrs Cuckoo. "How are you?"

Mrs Blue Tit told her she wasn't

"Excuse me," whispered Mrs Blue Tit timidly.

Mrs Wood Owl sleepily opened one eye.

"*Tu-whit, hoo-hoo-hoooooooooo*," she grunted grumpily. "Don't you know I like to sleep during the day time? What do you want?"

"I wonder," she began hesitantly.

very happy, and why. But Mrs Cuckoo was unable to help. She hadn't seen a nice cosy nesting box either.

"I never build a nest," Mrs Cuckoo told her. "I lay my eggs in other birds' nests. Why don't you do the same?"

Mrs Blue Tit was quite shocked, she liked to look after her own babies. But she thanked Mrs Cuckoo for her help, and Mrs Cuckoo was pleased.

Across the meadow was the lake. The sun was shining on it so brightly that it looked to be full of tiny gold pockets. Swimming in and out of the gold pockets was Mrs Duck.

"*Quack quack*," she called to Mrs Blue Tit. "What can I do for you?"

"Do you know of a nice cosy nesting box where I could build my nest?" Mrs Blue Tit asked her hopefully.

Mrs Duck thought for a moment. "There was one in Farmer Pybus's meadow, I seem to remember," she said. "But wait a minute, yes, I am sorry, it blew down in a gale. That was the only

one as far as I know."

"Oh, dear," sighed Mrs Blue Tit. "I am never going to find one."

"Do cheer up," quacked Mrs Duck. "If it is any help to you *I* build my nest on the ground. Why don't you do the same?"

"It would be much too hard for me," replied Mrs Blue Tit. "But thank you for your help."

"You're welcome," quacked Mrs Duck continuing her swim.

By this time Mrs Blue Tit was beginning to feel very tired. So she rested on the branches of a hazel tree. Suddenly the soft yellowy-brown catkins began to dance. It was the wind blowing them until they banged into one another, and the wind laughed.

"*Whooooooooooo, whoooooooooooo, whooooooooooo,*" he bellowed. "This is a fine day for spring." Then he noticed Mrs Blue Tit, her head tucked under her wing and breathing with *such* heavy sighs, because she was unhappy.

"We can't have this," called the kindly wind. "Whatever is the matter?"

And Mrs Blue Tit told him.

The wind chuckled. "Not to worry, come with me. Be happy! It is springtime."

Before Mrs Blue Tit realized what was happening the wind had gathered her up with a great puff and carried her to the Cherry Orchard.

Mrs Blue Tit couldn't believe her eyes, for there on one of the cherry trees was a tiny brown wooden nesting box. It had a small pointed roof and the door was a small round hole in the front. Mrs Blue Tit was just going to pop inside when she saw a head appear.

"There is someone inside," she cried. "I am too late."

"Wait and see who it is," teased the wind.

Then the someone came out. It was Mr Blue Tit.

"Welcome home," he said.

Mrs Blue Tit flew inside and, as you can imagine, it was as cosy as could be.

PADDY'S MAGIC PONY

Have you ever seen a leprechaun? In Ireland they say there are little men who dress all in green and who can do magic, and these are leprechauns.

One day Paddy was walking in a field near his home when he spotted a leprechaun walking through the long grass. Paddy crept silently up behind him and grabbed him round his waist.

The leprechaun cried out and began to struggle, but Paddy held on tight.

"Well, now, I seem to be caught," said the leprechaun, "but if you'll just be so kind as to let go, I'll be on my way."

"Not likely!" said Paddy. "Now I've caught you, you have to do something magic for me before I let you go. That's what leprechauns do."

"Ah, yes," said the leprechaun, stroking his whiskers, "I've a nice bag of gold here, but you mustn't look at it before you get home, or it will all turn into pebbles. Will that do?"

"No, thank you," said Paddy politely, "I've heard of that trick. It will all be pebbles anyway."

"Oh dear," sighed the leprechaun, "I can see you're too clever for me. What do you want then?"

"A pony," said Paddy firmly. "A beautiful white pony. That's what I want."

35

"Here goes, then," said the leprechaun, snapping his fingers. And there in front of them stood a lovely little white pony. "Now, will you let me go home?"

Paddy patted his pony's nose. "I think I'll call you Magic," he murmured happily. "Magic and I will take you home," he told the leprechaun.

"No need to trouble yourself," said the leprechaun.

But Paddy was already mounting his pony, still keeping a firm grip on the leprechaun.

"Well, if you'll just set me down by that oak tree over there," the leprechaun said, "you'll see my front door." He didn't like this at all.

Paddy rode to the tree and knelt down in front of the hole under it. "I can't see anything," he said, "this is just a rabbit burrow."

The leprechaun mopped his brow. "Don't you believe anything?" he asked crossly. "All right, walk round the other side of the tree."

Paddy did so, and as he stooped to look at the burrow there, he heard sounds of a jig being played on a fiddle, far below. Peering in, he saw lanterns flickering and tiny green men dancing.

"I believe you now," he said to the leprechaun as he released him. "Thank you for Magic."

The leprechaun slipped quickly down the hole, and Paddy rode proudly home on his white pony.

His mother came out of their cottage to meet him. She shook her head when Paddy told her how he came by the pony.

"It's no good, son, something bad will come of it. Those leprechauns are too tricky," she said. "It's a pity it's too late to take it to market, before it changes into a frog or vanishes altogether!"

Paddy fed and watered Magic and tied him up in the little shed beside the cottage, where the hens lived. "Goodnight, Magic," he said. "I hope you're still here in the morning!"

Next morning Paddy rushed straight out to the shed in his pyjamas, without waiting to get dressed. He opened the door, his hands trembling.

Magic hadn't vanished altogether, but he'd shrunk somewhat and he'd lost all his lovely white hair. To put it quite plainly, Magic had turned into a little pink piglet.

"It could be worse," said Paddy's mother. "We'll get a few shillings for him, at least."

Paddy wasn't to be cheered up. He was furious. "I'll catch that

slippery leprechaun again and make him give me my pony back!" he shouted.

When he was dressed, he took the little piglet to market and carried the money home to his mother, keeping a shilling for himself. Then he went over to Farmer O'Riley and asked if he could hire his big brown mare for the morning in return for his shilling. Farmer O'Riley agreed, so he led the mare to the tree where the leprechaun lived and tethered it by the stream, a few paces away.

He knelt down and peered again into the hole. There were the little green men, dancing down below. "Hey, leprechaun," he shouted. "Paddy Finnegan here would like a word with you!"

One of the leprechauns popped up, being careful to keep out of Paddy's reach. "You'll be a mite cross, I'm thinking," he said, grinning cheekily. "Well, you can't win every time."

"Not at all," said Paddy, "that little pony you gave me turned overnight into a big strong mare. I'm just on my way to market to sell her, and I've stopped by to thank you!"

The leprechaun's smile faded and he looked puzzled. "That's very nice," he said doubtfully.

"Don't you want to see?" asked Paddy. "She's tethered by the stream."

The leprechaun grinned again.

"A nice try, boy!" he said, "but I think it's a little piglet you've got over there!"

Just then, Farmer O'Riley's mare neighed. The leprechaun's smile vanished again and he looked even more puzzled. "Well, perhaps I will just have a peep," he said nervously, and wriggled out of the hole.

Paddy grabbed him straight away. "Got you again!" he shouted. "Now, give me my pony back."

The leprechaun groaned. "I'll change your big brown mare back to a pony then," he said, about to snap his fingers.

Paddy took hold of his hand.

"Not so fast," he said. "That's Farmer O'Riley's horse. I want *mine* back. And no more tricks, or I'll pour buckets of water into your hole, and float every one of you out!"

The leprechaun could see Paddy meant it. He snapped his fingers and there was Magic again, as beautiful as ever. "There you are now, and you've got the better of me this time, and no mistake," he said.

Paddy let the leprechaun go and mounted Magic. Then he rode back home, leading Farmer Riley's mare, and humming a jig as he went. This time he was going to keep his Magic pony!

Khaki Campbell, The Duck with the Loudest Quack

If you go through Wishing Wattle Woods, down the long brown lane, across the meadow with the yellowest buttercups, you will come to the green, green Silverdown River: the home of Khaki Campbell, the duck with the loudest quack.

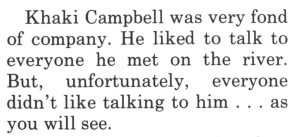

Khaki Campbell was very fond of company. He liked to talk to everyone he met on the river. But, unfortunately, everyone didn't like talking to him . . . as you will see.

One bright, gold, sunshiny after-noon Khaki Campbell swam in and out of the lily pads, through the swishing rushes and along the bank of the river looking for someone to talk to.

On the bank he saw Mr Water Rat grooming his whiskers after his afternoon swim.

"*Quack quack, quack quack*," greeted Khaki Campbell loudly. "Isn't it a lovely afternoon? *Quack quack, quack quack*."

Mr Rat hastily bent his head and held his claws over his ears until Khaki Campbell had finished quacking.

Then he said, "Oh my nose, and oh my whiskers, what a terrible noise. Why, it's louder than the moo of Farmer Pybus's cow, louder than the neigh of his horse, and far louder than the *cock-a-doodle-doo* of his cockerel. Please, please, go away."

Khaki Campbell bowed his head. He knew his quack was loud, but he just couldn't quack quietly. It was the way he was made. So he swam away from the water rat, and went in and out of the lily pads, through the swishing rushes and along the bank of the green, green Silverdown River, to see if he could find anyone else to talk to.

Then on the bank he saw a small brown mole hill. And as he watched Mr Mole's black velvet head popped out of the top. He climbed out and dusted down his black velvet coat.

"*Quack quack, quack quack*," cried Khaki Campbell. "Isn't it a lovely afternoon?"

Mr Mole jumped with alarm and held his little pink paws tightly against his head until Khaki Campbell had finished quacking.

"Oh my paws!" said Mr Mole. "What a terrible noise. I do be-

lieve it's louder than the moo of Farmer Pybus's cow, louder than the neigh of his horse, and far louder than the *cock-a-doodle-doo* of his cockerel. I think you should go away and leave me in peace."

Khaki Campbell bowed his little head and swam away. And once again he went in and out of the lily pads, through the swishing rushes and along the bank of the green, green Silverdown River looking for someone to talk to.

"Surely there must be someone," he said, shaking his little brown head. "Surely there must be someone who will like my quack."

Then, skimming over the waters of the green, green Silverdown River, he saw a party of swallows.

"*Quack quack, quack quack,* isn't it a lovely afternoon? *Quack, quack, quack.*"

The swallows quickly flew higher into the sky.

"Did you hear that terrible noise," said one. "It's louder than the moo of Farmer Pybus's cow, and louder than the neigh of his horse."

"Yes," agreed another swallow. "And I think it is even louder than the *cock-a-doodle-doo* of his cockerel."

And they all flew away.

Khaki Campbell bowed his little brown head and swam in and out

of the lily pads, through the swishing rushes and along the bank of the green, green Silverdown River, until he found a little place to rest. For he was very tired of looking for someone to talk to.

When he woke up it wasn't a sunshiny afternoon any more; it was nearly night time. The stars were just beginning to peep out and the moon was beginning to wake up too. It was rising over the tree tops.

"I wonder if the moon would talk to me," said Khaki Campbell to himself. "But I expect it's too far away to even hear my quacks." Then he noticed a large brown shape fly silently over the river and settle in a large oak tree.

Khaki Campbell swam over to see who it was. Two large bright yellow eyes blinked at him. It was Mr Owl.

"*Quack quack, quack quack,* isn't it a lovely evening? *Quack, quack, quack,*" went Khaki Campbell, feeling sure Mr Owl would talk to him.

Mr Owl nearly fell off the branch he was resting on.

"Oh my claws, and oh my

feathers!" he said. "What a terrible noise you make for such a little duck. Has anyone ever told you your quack is louder than the moo made by Farmer Pybus's cow, and louder than the neigh of his horse. And I'm sure it is louder than the *cock-a-doodle-doo* of his cockerel. Now, please go away, I want some peace and quiet."

Khaki Campbell didn't utter another quack. He swam quietly away, in and out of the lily pads and through the swishing rushes and sadly, and unhappily, along the bank of the green, green Silverdown River.

"No one will ever talk to me,"

And Farmer Pybus searched in all his pockets until he found the remains of his lunchtime sandwiches. He threw some to Khaki Campbell.

"*Quack quack, quack quack*, thank you very much," quacked Khaki Campbell. "*Quack, quack*."

What a lovely surprise, Farmer Pybus didn't put his hands over his ears, and say what a terrible noise. And he didn't even walk away. He watched Khaki Campbell eat all the bread.

"*Quack quack*," went Khaki Campbell. "That was nice, *quack quack*."

Farmer Pybus smiled every time

he said to himself. "I will never have a friend."

Then along the bank of the green, green Silverdown River he heard the sound of footsteps. It was Farmer Pybus, the one who had the cow, the horse, the cockerel, all of which didn't make a noise as loud as Khaki Campbell.

Farmer Pybus saw Khaki Campbell. "Hello, little duck," he said. "You are up late. Would you like a scrap of bread for your supper?"

he quacked, and nodded his head as though he was thinking something over. Then he said, "You are just the very one I have been looking for."

Khaki Campbell looked very surprised.

"I wonder," went on Farmer Pybus, "if you would come to live on my pond in the farmyard. You see I'm a little deaf, and when anyone calls to see me I can never hear their knock. But if you were to quack when someone called everything would be fine, because I can hear *you*."

"*Quack quack, quack quack*," cried Khaki Campbell. "I will come straight away." And he hopped onto the bank and followed the farmer, quacking happily all the way.

The pond was only small, but it had lily pads and swishing rushes, and green, green water like the Silverdown River, so Khaki Campbell felt at home.

And when anyone called to see Farmer Pybus, Khaki Campbell would say, "*Quack quack, quack quack*," at the top of his voice. Farmer Pybus soon answered the door.

Then he would say to the visitor, "Come and meet my little duck, Khaki Campbell, for without him I wouldn't have known you were here. He is the duck with the loudest quack. And I'm very proud of him."

45

The little airy fairy man
Loves to hide wherever he can,
Under a stile or in a pansy's fan,
Inside a buttercup, inside a shoe,
Anywhere small and secret will do!
Beside a daisy, behind a door,
He'll hide where he's never hidden before!
The little airy fairy man
Loves to hide wherever he can,
And no one even knows his name,
Where he's going to and whence he came.

Can *you* find the airy fairy man?

THE LITTLE AIRY FAIRY MAN

The cat with odd eyes

This is the story of Mingle, a little, dusty white kitten who was just seven weeks old.

His mother was an alley cat and she had four other kittens as well as Mingle to feed and care about.

Mingle and his four brothers and sisters enjoyed life in the busy alley ways of Dewsbury town. There was so much to learn about: lessons on how to raid dustbins and finding the best hiding places in garden sheds.

The older cat cousins would often take Mingle and his brothers and sisters on early morning outings to gather cream from milk bottles on doorsteps. Then they had trips to the park and midnight feasts through open larder windows. It was all so exciting that Mingle wished for nothing else.

One evening, down in the musty coal cellar which was their home, they sat in a circle eating fish bones.

Mingle's mother sat there too, but she was not eating. Suddenly, she called them all closer and said, "There is something I have to tell you, my little ones."

"Oh, is it something nice?" shouted the kittens.

The grey mother cat sat back against a plank of wood and closed her eyes. When she opened them again their dreamy blue colour seemed to pierce the dark gloom of the cellar.

"Well," she sighed, "it all depends on how you look at it." She leaned forward. "The time has come for you all to leave home!"

The kittens moved uncomfortably and murmured among themselves.

Mingle was the first to speak. "Why do we have to leave home? We like it here."

"There are better homes than this one, real homes," said his mother. "An alley cat has a very hard life at times." She went on to explain about warm sitting rooms and soft arm-chairs, and kind owners. "If you live in a real home you feed on meat and fish and fresh milk," she told them.

"But I like our early morning outings with Uncle Whiskers," argued Mingle. "He *always* knows which houses get fresh cream."

"Ah, but that is stealing." His mother frowned through the dusty darkness. "If you live with a human family as their house pet you are *given* the cream. It's even poured into a bowl for you. No trouble at all," she laughed.

The young kittens sat up and took a new interest. Milk? Free? *And* poured

into a bowl? It all seemed too good to be true.

They all spoke at once: about meat and milk and fireside mats.

By the end of the evening they were all looking forward to a new life with a new owner; all of them except one, and that one was Mingle.

Mingle had a secret worry. His eyes were green and blue. That is not to say that both of them were green flecked with blue. Or even blue flecked with green. It was not quite as simple as that; Mingle had one green eye, and one blue eye.

The other cats had not remarked on his odd eyes, because alley cats do not really care about such unimportant things. But Mingle could not help wondering what human people would think. He could not bear it if they thought he was ugly, or different to his handsome brothers.

Early the next morning Mingle went out to find a puddle in the street where he sat looking at his reflection. He stared into the muddy water and thought hard about himself. Fluffy white coat, a bit dusty maybe, but his coat was thick and glossy, and he had a long tail that could swish hard, plump little pink paws and perky pointed ears. His reflection wavered as he peered closer into the depths of the puddle. Long silvery whiskers touched the water and he drew back to twitch a velvet-soft nose. He looked again and his eyes met their own mirror in the dark water.

He gasped, "One blue eye, and one green eye! I *am* different, not like the other alley cats at all."

The small white kitten wandered back along the street to meet his mother, just as she was herding the other kittens into line, ready for

their journey to the pet shop.

At the pet shop door the mother cat gave all her family damp, fond cat-kisses and then quickly marched away. She hated leaving them, but it was for their own good. Life had certainly been hard for her, a stray alley cat, and she wanted a better, easier life for her loved ones.

"I wonder what sort of homes we will get," miaowed one of the shaking kittens.

"Well, I want a home with children in it," said a tabby sister.

"And I want a home with soft cushions on the chairs," said her ginger brother.

Mingle did not speak.

Before long the manager of the shop came to the door and picked up the kittens. But Mingle did not get picked up!

Mingle had run to hide behind a dustbin . . .and there he stayed!

Later that day the lone white kitten watched from the street as his brothers and sisters played in the straw in the pet shop window. He trembled a little as he peered round the dustbin at them. They looked so happy and safe in the shop.

"I wonder if I should have gone with them after all," he sighed.

Mingle wandered down the street, not knowing the way back to the familiar alley ways where he had lived all his short life. As he passed the big glass windows of a furniture store his eyes looked away from their reflection; odd eyes, one green and one blue.

The shock came when Mingle tried to cross the road.

One white paw had already left the curb when he felt the scruff of his neck being clamped between powerful jaws. Then he was set gently down in a shop doorway.

A large, red-brown dog stood over him, speaking in a low, but firm voice. "I had to save you like that, or you would have been knocked down. The traffic is busy at this time of day, you know." He blinked large brown eyes. "I do hope I didn't hurt you."

"No, but you scared me," said Mingle. "I did not realise the town roads were dangerous. Thank you, big dog."

"Call me Sam," replied the dog. "My master calls me Sam."

"Ooooh, have you got a real, human master?" gasped the cat.

"Yes," said Sam. "He can't see very well now that he is old. I help him . . . I lead the way, you know." The big brown animal studied the little kitten for a while, then said, "My master has been wanting to buy a white kitten for a long time now, but the walk down to the pet shop is too far, what with all that traffic, and his eyes growing weak."

Mingle suddenly felt very happy, and his worried, white face lost its frown as he nodded and followed Sam along the street to a big, old house.

As they went in through the front door Mingle met his new master and he knew then that he had found a good kind home: the answer to a kitten's dream.

The old man loved Mingle as soon as he touched the soft, white fur, and heard with glad ears the friendly, happy cat-purrs.

And Sam, the dog, gave up his favourite fireside chair to their special, tiny guest.

That evening, Mingle sat on red cushions by a big log fire, and the lights from the fire were reflected, dancing, in his eyes. Odd eyes! One green and one blue. Eyes that looked strangely beautiful, and contented with the beginnings of a new and wonderful life.

ANIMAL HOMES

THE BEAVER

Using branches and twigs, beavers build a strong dam, or wall, across a river. This dam stops the water flowing down the river so that the beavers have a quiet pond in which to make their home. A beaver house is called a lodge, and it is also made from twigs and branches bound together with mud. They look like floating mounds, and have a dry room inside, so that the beavers are safe and warm through the winter.

THE HERMIT CRAB

The hermit crab has a soft body so, to protect itself from its enemies, it lives in a shell. A discarded sea shell becomes the crab's home, and it's a comical sight to see the crab dragging the shell along the sea bed. When the crab grows, it simply crawls into a larger shell and makes a new home there.

THE RABBIT

The wild rabbit lives deep under the ground in tunnels or burrows. The rabbits dig a narrow main tunnel deep into the ground, with a 'room' at the end of it, and then they dig other smaller tunnels branching from the main one. Here the rabbits can hide from their enemies, rear their young and store food.

THE SWALLOW

The swallow rarely makes its nest in a tree like other birds, it prefers to make its nest on houses, barns or other buildings. It makes a saucer shaped nest of mud, grass and feathers and attaches this nest under the eaves of a house or the beam in a barn or other farm building.

THE DRAGON -O-BUS

Once upon a time, in the mountains of goodness-knows-where, there lived a dragon who was very sad.

"Oh dear!" he said to himself one day, as he lay in the sunshine blowing smoke-rings, "I do wish that something exciting would happen. Why, I've been here for three hundred years and only one fairy prince has been to fight me. He only came here by mistake and he ran away as soon as he saw me."

The dragon gave a deep sigh and a tear ran down his orange cheek. Then he chewed a lump from a nearby boulder, blew a few more smoke-rings and then he went to sleep, for there was simply nothing else for a dragon to do.

A few days later, when he was awaking from his nap, he was surprised to hear a voice.

"It's all right, Woffles," said the voice. "He won't hurt us."

The dragon opened one eye and saw an elf with his arm around a trembling mouse. He opened his other eye, pleased that there was someone to talk to at last.

When the elf saw that the dragon was awake, he smiled at him.

"Hello, Mr Dragon, I hope that we didn't wake you. We are trying to find our way to the other side of the mountains."

"Hello!" replied the dragon. "My name is Rufus the Red. What are your names, and why are you going to the other side of the mountains?"

"We are going to seek our fortunes. My name is Merryone and this is my friend Woffles. We used to drive our bus in Elf Land, but last week it fell into hundreds of pieces so we haven't got jobs any longer. We hope to find a treasure so that we can buy another bus."

Rufus shook his head. "The land

beyond the mountains is full of danger. There are giants there even bigger than I am! Kaarl the eagle told me about them. They could swallow you both in one gulp!"

"Oh dear!" said Merryone in alarm. "But what *can* we do if we don't seek our fortune there?"

"I can give you some gold dust," Rufus offered. "I've got a little which I don't need — it tastes rather odd. Perhaps you should ask the advice of the Wise Woman about how you could get another bus for Elf Land."

"It was the Wise Woman who told us that we would find what we were looking for here in the mountains," Merryone explained. "If we take some of your gold, Rufus, what can we do for you in return?"

"What I would like more than anything in the world," said Rufus, "would be to go with you to Elf Land. I am so lonely living here all alone." A tear dropped to the ground, splashing the elf and the mouse so that they had to leap to safety.

"Of course you may come with us, Rufus. Only do stop crying or you'll make us soaking wet!"

Rufus was so happy that he blew fifteen smoke-rings, one after another, and singed Woffles' whiskers. Then Merryone was shown the gold·dust and he filled his pockets with it, and then the three of them walked together back along the track which led to Elf Land.

They had not gone very far before Merryone stopped and mopped his brow, for the day was very hot and they had walked a long way that morning.

"I'm so tired," sighed Woffles, stretching his small legs.

"I'm not," said Rufus. "I am very strong. Why don't you climb onto my back and ride into Elf Land?"

So Merryone and Woffles climbed onto the dragon's back and rode the rest of the journey in style, until at last they reached the village. There they saw Mother Soapsuds, the lady who did the washing for the people who lived in Elf Land. She was walking along with a big bundle of washing in her arms.

"Hello, there!" called Merryone, for he was a friendly person.

But when Mother Soapsuds saw him and saw Rufus, she screamed, dropped the washing and then ran wildly down the road, full of fear.

"Please don't be afraid," called

Woffles. "Rufus is our friend, he won't hurt you. If you like you may ride on his back too, your washing must be very heavy."

When she saw that Merryone and Woffles were so happy, Mother Soapsuds gathered up her washing and climbed alongside them on the dragon's back.

Next they met Mr. Sticky from the sweetshop, Wizard Knowall and the old lady who sold toffee apples. They all climbed onto Rufus' back for a ride.

"Well, well," said Wizard Knowall. "This is an excellent idea. Why doesn't your friend Rufus stay in our village and make this his regular job? It has been very hard on the feet of the old people here since Merryone's bus fell to pieces. We could do with some kind of transport from one end of the village to the other, and I'm sure that the Village Council will approve."

Rufus was almost bursting with pride at the idea. He thought that it was wonderful.

When the party reached the main street of the village, however, the people were full of terror when they saw a dragon walking along the road. They all ran into their houses and locked the doors.

But when they peeped out of their

bedroom windows and saw their own villagers riding on the dragon's back they lost their fear and came out to see.

"Oh, look, Mummy!" said one small child. "It's a dragon-o-bus."

"I want to have a ride," said another.

"There you are, Rufus," said Merryone, patting his friend on the head. "How would you like to be our dragon-o-bus?"

"I'd like it very much," said Rufus, grinning from ear to ear.

So that is the story of how Rufus the dragon replaced the village bus in the land of the elves. Merryone and Rufus built a beautiful house for them all, and they made wonderful pies for Rufus to eat. The school children gave Rufus sweets and buns when they were taken to school and on picnics. They all had great fun, playing games on his long tail, and he was never lonely and unhappy again.

The Meadow alarm clock

Across the magic meadow,
By the fairy stream,
Lives a thimble-sized fellow,
Completely dressed in green.

His job is to wake the flowers,
On every summer's day,
So that each petal coat is gleaming
When the sun comes out to play.

At evening time, when it goes dark,
He visits every flower in sight,
To see they're all quite happy,
And bid them a gentle 'goodnight'.

A DAY AT THE FARM

The sun began to rise over the hill. The birds started to sing and down on the farm in the valley:

The roosters crowed and were awake.

The cows mooed and were awake.

The pigs grunted and were awake.

The horses neighed and were awake.

The ducks quacked and were awake.

The hens clucked and were awake.

Sally, who lived on the farm, yawned and woke up. Sally got up quickly. There was much work to be done. The animals wanted their breakfast. Sally dressed quickly and had her breakfast. She went into the farmyard to feed the animals.

"Good morning, roosters," said Sally, "enjoy your breakfast."

"*Cock-a-doodle-do*," said the roosters.

"Good morning, cows," said Sally, "enjoy your breakfast."

"*Moo*," said the cows.

"Good morning, pigs," said Sally, "enjoy your breakfast."

"*Grunt*," said the pigs.

"Good morning, horses," said Sally, "enjoy your breakfast."

"*Neigh*," said the horses.

"Good morning, ducks," said Sally, "enjoy your breakfast."

"*Quack*," said the ducks.

"Good morning, hens," said Sally, "enjoy your breakfast."

"*Cluck*," said the hens.

Now all the animals have been fed.

Sally milked the cows and collected the eggs. She put the milk and the eggs in her basket and set off to market.

Along the road Sally met Mr. Dough, the baker.

"Good morning, Sally, any bread today?" asked Mr. Dough.

"Two loaves, please," said Sally.

Sally put the bread in her basket with the eggs and milk. Soon Sally reached the market, and a big jolly lady bought all Sally's eggs and milk. Sally set off home.

After lunch Sally went to the fields to help her father with the haymaking. They worked very hard. Soon it was evening and the animals grew tired.

The roosters stopped crowing and went to sleep.

The cows stopped mooing and went to sleep.

The pigs stopped grunting and went to sleep.

The horses stopped neighing and went to sleep.

The ducks stopped quacking and went to sleep.

The hens stopped clucking and went to sleep.

Sally got into her little bed, yawned, and went to sleep. The farm birds stopped singing and went to sleep. The farm in the valley was fast asleep and, last of all, the sun sank below the hill, and the only things awake were the big round moon, the twinkling stars and the wise old owl in the oak tree.

THE SNOWY WHITE ROBIN

"Wake up! Wake up! Spring is here," chorused the daffodils, raising their golden trumpets up towards the sun.

"Why, I believe it is!" yawned Donald Dormouse, unrolling himself lazily as he rubbed his eyes.

Everywhere the air was full of twitterings from tiny feathered throats. And dazzling sunbeams darted in and out of the hazelnut tree, setting the catkins a-dancing.

Yes, the daffodils were right – Spring *had* arrived.

High up in the hazelnut tree sat Papa Robin, eyeing his three baby fledglings as they bounced up and down on a bendy branch.

"Now, my fine sons," he chirped, "you are ready to face the big wide world." And he puffed out his handsome red breast with pride.

"But, Papa, how will the world know that we *are* robins?" piped up Reggie. "We haven't red waistcoats like you."

And he and his brothers, Roly and Robbie, looked glumly down at their speckled brown breasts.

"*Tic*, *tic*, have patience, my children," scolded Papa Robin. "There are many prowling creatures down below just waiting to pounce on timid little birds. Your speckled breasts will not be so easy to spot. Now do you understand?"

Reggie, Roly and Robbie nodded their fluffy heads. "Yes, Papa," they twittered. "But how long do we have to wait?"

"Not long, my sons. As soon as your wings have grown strong, the hot summer sun will change the colour of your waistcoats to red. Come on now, it's time for another flying lesson."

The young robins grew and grew as the days lengthened. And then one day it happened.

"Look, look!" chirped Reggie, pointing to his breast.

And sure enough a rich red-brown feather peeped out from amongst his speckles.

His brothers looked wide-eyed at Reggie, and then they looked eagerly downwards. But there wasn't a sign of any new feathers on their waistcoats.

A week went by before Roly chirped out happily. "I've got one too, just like yours, Reggie." And there was the red feather – right in the middle.

The two brothers turned to Robbie, who was now feeling sad and forlorn. "Cheer up, Robbie," they cheeped. "It's your turn next."

Day followed day but there was still no sign of Robbie's new coat. True, his speckles had started to disappear but, if anything, his breast was getting paler.

Reggie and Roly had grown lots of red feathers now, and they hopped about, looking very important. But poor Robbie – his breast had turned a pure white. And he was *so* unhappy.

His brothers looked at him with concern. "He can't be our real brother," declared Reggie, "or else he would have a red breast like us."

"You're right," replied Roly. "We'd better ignore him."

And they flew off to play tag with the blue-tits.

The months passed quickly by and the leaves fluttered down to form a red, yellow and golden carpet. Autumn had come and it had started to get cold.

Up on a bare branch huddled Robbie. "*Br-rrr*. How will I keep warm when Winter is here?" he sighed. "I've no red breast to lay my head on."

At that moment the Tuck-Them-Up Fairy glided past. She had been flying around to make sure all the creatures were ready for their winter sleep.

Donald Dormouse was snuggly bedded down in his cosy nest, snoring away peacefully. The squirrels were already high up in their drey. And even

Harry Hedgehog had crawled under a huge pile of leaves, and rolled himself into a prickly pin-cushion.

So the sight of what looked like a ball of cottonwool in the hazelnut tree surprised the Tuck-Them-Up Fairy. She just had to go back and make sure.

"My goodness!" she exclaimed. "It's a snow white robin – you poor thing."

Robbie blinked at the fairy, and a big tear rolled down his cheek. "I'm so afraid," he trembled. "Because the snow will soon fall and I'll freeze and die."

"But I can't allow that to happen," cried the fairy. "My task is to see that all Nature's creatures are kept warm and tucked-up for the winter." And she put on her thinking-cap and thought and thought.

Suddenly her face lit up and she gave a squeal of glee. "Of course, of course," she chuckled. "I remember now . . . listen."

Robbie's eyes brightened as he cocked his head on one side and listened to the fairy's story.

"Long, long ago," the fairy began, "something very wonderful happened to a beautiful maiden when she received a kiss. And you remind me of her. Her name was Snow White."

Robbie looked puzzled. "But what is a kiss?" he chirped.

The Fairy smiled. "Close your eyes and you'll find out," she beamed.

And, moving closer to the snowy white bird, she kissed him softly on the cheek.

At first Robbie didn't know what had happened. But as he opened his eyes, he suddenly felt very bashful. And then he started to blush.

His cheek felt warm and then the pinky blush crept down under his chin and onto his breast.

Then, as the fairy looked on, it changed first to a rosy hue, and then slowly into a deep, rich, orangy-red.

Robbie looked down at his beautiful waistcoat and chirped happily. "I've got a red breast, a real red breast!"

"Wait a moment," said the fairy. "We must make sure it stays red." And she tapped Robbie's breast very, very, gently with the star on the end of her wand.

"There, now you'll always have a red breast," she beamed. "And you'll never feel the cold."

"Oh, thank you, thank you, kind fairy," cheeped Robbie. And he buried his head in the soft feathers of his breast, and went sound asleep.

WHO HELPS THE FARMER?

The farmer keeps a lot of animals. He always makes sure that they are happy and have plenty of the right food to eat because he needs them to give him produce to sell at the markets.

COWS

The farmer's cows like to graze in the fields in summer, but in bad weather and at night they stay in the byre where the farmer gives them hay to eat. In return they give the farmer milk to sell so that we can have milk, butter and cheese.

SHEEP

Sheep like to live on the hills, as they do not mind the cold and can stay outside all year round. In winter they grow a thick fleece to protect them from the harsh winds, but when spring comes this is too warm for them and the farmer gives them a bath before he shears off their fleeces to make your woolly jumpers.

CHICKENS

Chickens like to scratch about the farmyard looking for corn to eat, and the farmer throws the corn on the ground for them to pick up. In return they lay eggs for you to eat for your breakfast.

DOGS

Most farmers keep dogs to round up the sheep and cattle without frightening them. They can bring the animals to him and guide them safely away when the farmer has fed them. A farm dog eats meat, and he enjoys a bone. A farmer and his dog are the best of friends.

HORSES

Although in olden times the farmer could not look after his farm without his horses, now many farmers use big tractors instead. A few farmers like to keep their friends the horses on the farm. They eat hay and oats and the farmer uses two shire horses to plough his fields ready for planting crops to feed the other animals, or to grow into corn which makes our bread.

CATS

There is usually a family of cats on a farm. They catch mice and rats which would otherwise eat the farmer's grain. The farmer's wife feeds them with scraps, and they live in the barns and animal pens where it is warm.

The Too-Helpful GIANT

It was a very hot morning on a smallish Greek island when the world was young and green. Demetrios lay on the ground staring up through the rough branches of an olive tree, feeling very sleepy and tired of looking after his father's stupid sheep. The sky above him was so blue that it was almost not blue at all, and the mountains grew so tall that they nearly reached it.

Demetrios picked up his little pipes and started to play a dreamy tune, a strange tune that ran through his head unasked, although he did not remember hearing it before.

Suddenly, out of the corner of his eye, he thought he saw the great brown rocks on the mountainside moving. He stopped playing and scrambled to his feet. Nothing there but a mountain goat. He began to play again and there was a great rumbling noise as part of the mountain seemed to come away and move towards him, taking the shape of a man.

Demetrios did not wait. He was not the champion runner of the local boys for nothing. He ran. But there was a thudding behind him, and the boy found himself picked up and wafted

71

above the olive tree and the craggy rocks. He wriggled and shouted but something held him tightly, and he was set down on a smooth, humpy platform, halfway to the sky.

After a moment Demetrios realised that the platform was the hand of a giant for, as he looked upwards, he saw a huge face with eyebrows and a beard like bushes in springtime, and a mouth like a rocky cave.

Out of this mouth came a deep, thunderous voice. "Running away?"

Demetrios scrambled to his feet. His knees were knocking together with fright, but he was of royal blood and he was not going to show his fear, even to a giant.

"I'm not frightened of you," he yelled in a voice that came out as a shrill squeak.

"Not afraid?" The huge fingers moved towards him.

"Not much," Demetrios admitted, thinking that perhaps in the circumstances it was wiser to be honest. "But you had better put me down. My father is a king and he has an army of warriors."

"A king?" The giant shook with laughter, which was dangerous for Demetrios as he nearly fell off his hand. He looked at the boy's brown working tunic. "You are only a shepherd."

"Even a king's son must work," Demetrios said, more bravely because he could see that the giant did not know everything. "My father believes that everyone must work and he has so many sheep that we all have to take turns to look after them. As far as you can see are my father's sheep."

And it was true. There were hundreds of sheep all over the plain that led down to the dark sea with the square-sailed ships on it.

"I see," said the giant thoughtfully. "Then why does he live in such a poor sort of palace, if that is your father's palace over there?"

"That's our city," replied Demetrios, somewhat indignantly. "It's not poor. It is a fine city, but my father has ordered the walls to be built up higher because we are always being attacked by enemies."

"I could build them up better than your little citizens," said the giant boastfully. "I, Ouros, will show you."

Before Demetrios could say or do anything — which would have been dificult anyway, because he was perched on the open hand of the giant — he found himself being moved towards the city.

In ten strides, Ouros was towering over the gates of the city. From below him came shouts and screams from the terrified citizens, and the king himself came out of the palace wanting to know what was making the city grow dark so suddenly.

Then he looked up and up and he saw the great face of Ouros suspended, as it seemed in the sky. Then the king saw the huge body and the hand with his son on it and he panicked.

"Attack!" he ordered his soldiers who were near. "Rush him with swords and lances. Hurl stones. Save Demetrios!"

They ran to obey, scrambling through the gates and hurrying up the stone staircases to the top of the walls, falling over each other in their haste. Then a shower of stones and javelins was let fly at the giant, to whom they were like pin-pricks. But one stone just missed Demetrios.

"Ouros, put me down," he shouted. "I must stop them."

Without a word, the great hand set Demetrios down on top of the wall.

"Stop shooting javelins and throwing stones," Demetrios commanded. "Ouros will not hurt us. He wants to help us build our city walls, don't you, Ouros?"

The great head nodded and, stooping down, the giant began to pile stones on each other like a little boy playing with bricks. All the citizens came out of hiding to watch and they cried out in amazement as the wall grew before their eyes. Long before it was dark, half the city had a new high and strong wall.

The king was delighted.

"Demetrios, my son," he said, "you were quite right. What a wonderful creature he is. Even the gods themselves could hardly work as fast. I will see what he wants as a reward."

He disappeared into the palace, put on his best cloak with the gold embroidery which he wore to receive ambassadors to the city and went to the main gate where Ouros had sat down to rest and talk to the interested citizens.

"I wish to know, mighty Ouros," the king began respectfully, "what you would like to receive in payment for your labour. I will give you half my treasury . . ."

"What use would gold be to me?" asked Ouros, but not unkindly.

"You can marry my daughter," said the king, but rather doubtfully because he could not imagine what she would say about it, and because the giant was so very large.

Ouros shook his shaggy head. "I don't want to marry your daughter or anyone else. She is too small to

make any sort of a wife for me. I will be quite happy if you let me sleep in front of your gates on this soft grass and bring me milk to drink and bread to eat."

"Certainly," agreed the king at once, and he ordered fifty barrels of wine and fifty bowls of milk and a hundred loaves of bread to be brought, which was more than a quarter of the store in the city.

Ouros ate all the bread and drank the wine and milk, wiping his beard and exclaiming how very good it all was. Then he stretched himself out on the ground and fell asleep.

Next day he finished the walls, and half the food and wine. The king was most grateful to Ouros, even if he was getting rather worried about the food supplies. All the same, it was very useful to have a giant at hand.

Demetrios and his friends did not have to look after sheep because Ouros could keep an eye on the whole plain at once, and so they had plenty of time for mischief. The soldiers did not need to fight, no enemy would attack a city which had a giant permanently outside its gates. The workmen had no building to do. The fisherman did not need to go out in their square-sailed boats because the giant waded out into the sea and, scooping up fish in his huge hands, threw them down at the gates, a shining heap.

You would think that everyone would be very happy. There was nothing to do but bake bread for Ouros and milk the cows and sheep and wait for the new crops to grow to have more corn for bread. But, even when the world was young, plants took their own time to grow. Every-

not get food from outside.

"What are we to do?" the king asked his council at last.

"Get rid of Ouros," they said. "Demetrios brought him here. He must send him back."

"But how can I do that?" Demetrios asked, his dark eyes wide open. "He is a giant, and, although he has been well-inclined towards us up to now, he might get very angry and destroy us all if we told him we did not want him here."

"Go to the Wise Woman," the king said. "She will tell you what to do."

Early the next morning, Demetrios set off, rather unwillingly, to find the cave of the Wise Woman in the mountains. It was lonely among the echoing hills and the stony paths hurt the boy's feet, but he kept on until he came to a narrow valley where gloomy trees grew close together and no birds were singing. Then Demetrios, who was very frightened, pulled in his belt and walked carefully until he heard the sound of a voice humming to itself. It was a harsh, tuneless sound and it came from the entrance to a small cave.

Then a voice called, "Come, Demetrios."

He was startled that whoever it was should know his name. He climbed up through the ferns and damp mosses, and soon he was inside a dark, dismal cave. There was a horrible smell and when he got used to the dim light he could see an old, old woman crouched over a big pot with yellow smoke swirling around her.

"I know why you have come," she said. "You want to send Ouros, the giant, back to where he came from."

"But we can't tell him that we do

one was becoming bored and restless. They were bored with not working and bored with looking at their own faces because no one from outside would venture near the city. And, above all, they were bored with eating fish because Ouros had eaten and drunk everything else and they could not want him any more," Demetrios said, getting used to the old woman knowing everything without being told.

There was silence, apart from the hissing of the pot and the crackling of the fire.

"What were you doing when he first appeared?" the Wise Woman asked at last.

Demetrios thought hard. "I was lying under an olive tree, watching the sheep."

"Yes, yes," she said impatiently, "but you must have been doing something else, something that was the key . . ."

"I was playing my pipes."

The Wise Woman jumped up and did a weird little dance. "I have it, I have it! You must remember the tune and play it backwards."

Demetrios's face fell. "But, I can't remember it. I had never heard the tune before."

The Wise Woman gave him a little push that sent him out of the cave. "Go and remember," was all she said.

Demetrios hurried back, trying out different tunes as he went. He reported to his father what the Wise Woman said, took up his pipes and began to play.

Everyone else helpfully took out their pipes to try to discover the right tune and the noise was unbearable, so much so that Demetrios began to walk right away from the city by himself. He climbed up towards the very olive tree where he first saw Ouros, lay under it and stared up through its branches. It was hot and he began, very slowly, to play a dreamy little tune, that same, strange tune that he had played before. He stopped. Carefully he tried to play it backwards, and it was not easy. After many mistakes, it began to come right, and he could feel the ground shaking under him.

"Stop, Demetrios, stop," thundered Ouros's voice and he strode towards the boy.

But Demetrios did not stop and he did not look at the giant. He thought of the people of the city with nothing to do and nothing to eat but fish, and he kept on playing until the giant had gone past him and melted once more into the great brown rocks of the hillside.

The king, Demetrios and all the people used to stare curiously up at the crags that looked just like a huge man, and then they went on fishing and growing crops and fighting their enemies. And Demetrios watched his father's sheep and dreamt under the olive trees but, just in case he should forget and play that dreamy little tune again, he dropped his pipes into the depths of the dark blue sea.

THE ELEPHANT-CATCHING KITTEN

"I wish I could catch an elephant!" sighed Kerry, as he sharpened his claws on the garden wall.

"Nonsense!" said his mother, Dinah. "Kittens were made to catch mice and birds. Now wash your face and forget all about big-game hunting. I shan't let you watch television again if it gives you silly ideas."

Kerry dreamily washed his ginger face and his white paws. Elephants! Long, swinging trunks and wide backs to ride. Much more fun than mice or birds. Easier to catch too, because they could not fly, or even run very fast. Maybe one lives in the jungly part at the end of the garden!

"Where are you going?" asked

Dinah, as she gave her shiny, black fur a last lick.

"Just looking for elephants," said Kerry, and he stalked off down the garden path.

"Oh dear!" sighed his mother. "He's just like his father, too big for his basket. He will have to be taught a lesson."

She thought hard and then went into the house to explore.

All through tea Kerry talked about elephants. He thought he had seen elephant tracks in the mud by the pond. He was almost sure he had heard an elephant blowing its nose behind the oak tree. He was quite sure he had nearly seen an elephant through the bushes.

Dinah had heard enough.

"Kerry," she said, "you may be right. I think I heard an elephant in the hall cupboard. It must be hiding."

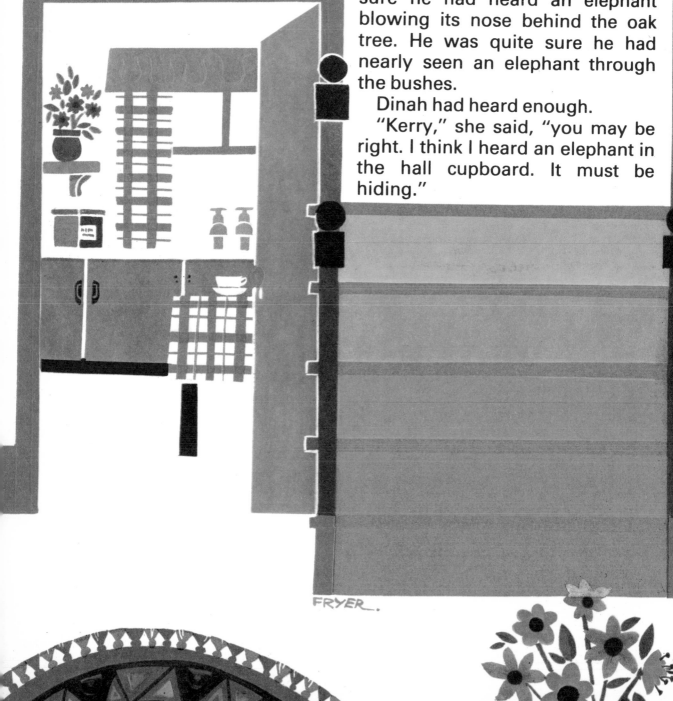

FRYER.

Kerry's whiskers quivered with excitement.

"I'll catch it right away," he whispered and began to creep towards the kitchen door.

"Now, Kerry, you know I don't like elephants. Just give me a few minutes to run upstairs out of the way," said Dinah.

She quickly slipped out of the kitchen, but not upstairs. Instead, she quietly padded to the back of the hall cupboard and crouched down in the dark. She made sure she was well hidden behind the vacuum cleaner which lived there with its long tube when it was not being used.

While he was waiting, Kerry sharpened his claws on the leg of the kitchen table, just in case. Then tail in the air, he began his elephant hunt. Very softly, on tiptoe, he nosed the kitchen door open. Nose twitching, he crept slowly across the hall, hoping the elephant was asleep.

He paused and listened outside the cupboard door. Not a sound!

He gently pushed the door open and peeped inside. It was very dark. He stepped in and carefully peered round.

Suddenly he saw the long tube on the floor. The elephant's trunk! He must be lying down asleep. This should be easy!

Kerry slowly stretched out his paw and patted the elephant's trunk. Nothing happened. He patted it a bit harder. Still nothing happened. Feeling braver, Kerry went up close and sniffed the end of the the tube.

"*Brrrrr — rrrrr — grrrrr — rrrrr!*" The elephant woke up.

Kerry, forgetting how easy it was to catch an elephant, leaped into the air and fled to his basket, his fur standing on end. He hid under his blanket and hoped the elephant would not come after him.

In the hall cupboard, Dinah pressed her paw on the vacuum cleaner button and the elephant went quiet. She crept out and went upstairs for a sleep.

As for Kerry, he never mentioned catching elephants again.

THE HOUSE THAT JACK BUILT

This is the house that Jack built.

This is the Malt
That lay in the House that Jack built.

This is the Cat
That scolded the Rat.

This is the Dog
That ran after the Cat.

This is the Cow with the crumpled horn,
That chased the Dog.

This is the Maiden all forlorn,
That milked the Cow with the crumpled horn.

This is the Man all tattered and torn,
That kissed the Maiden all forlorn.

This is the Priest all shaven and shorn
That married the Man all tattered and torn,
That kissed the Maiden all forlorn.

This is the Cock that crowed in the morn,
That awakened the Priest all shaven and shorn.

So here is a picture of the wedding morn,
Which shows the cock which crowed at dawn,
That wakened the Priest all shaven and shorn,
That married the Man all tattered and torn,
That kissed the Maiden all forlorn,
That milked the Cow with the crumpled horn,
That chased the Dog,
That ran after the Cat,
That scolded the Rat,
That ate the Malt,
That lay in the House that Jack built.

THE GOLDEN MONEY TREE

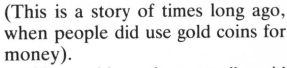

ONCE there was a boy named Richard, who was very fond of telling little lies to his sister Joanna. He thought it great fun to tell her all kinds of things that were not really true. And she, being much younger, believed every word Richard said.

One day Richard was busy doing his school homework, and little Joanna was waiting patiently for him to finish so that they could go out and play in the garden.

On the table were three little gold coins, given to Richard by his grandparents for being so clever at school.

(This is a story of times long ago, when people did use gold coins for money).

"How shiny they are," said Joanna, picking up the coins. "Will you give me one, Richard?"

"Leave them alone," said Richard. "I have to take them along to the bank to make them grow."

"How can a bank make them grow?" asked Joanna.

"The bank clerks plant them in a garden and carefully water them until they sprout into plants," Richard replied. "Then, about a year later, little trees grow and their leaves turn into gold coins which all fall to the ground. But don't bother me with your silly questions, Joanna, if you want me to finish work and go out to play with you."

"All right, Richard," said Joanna. She jumped down from her chair at the table and hurried into the garden.

Soon afterwards, Joanna was back in the house, and her eyes were sparkling wth joy and excitement.

"Do you know what I've done, with the money, Richard?" she asked. "I planted it in the garden and watered it, and now if the sun shines it will grow into golden money trees."

"What? You must be joking, you silly thing," gasped Richard.

"No, I'm not," replied Joanna. "I've really and truly planted the money in the garden so as to make it grow, and you will have a whole lot more."

"Oh dear, why must you believe all the things I tell you?" said Richard, hurriedly leaving his school work. "Show me exactly where you planted the money."

Richard pushed Joanna out into the garden, hoping she would remember where she had buried the golden coins.

But, alas, little Joanna had quite forgotten, and she had smoothed over the soil so neatly that there was no sign of the place.

"I must find it," said Richard.

"But why don't you leave it where it is?" Joanna asked. "You told me that was how the banks made golden money trees grow."

"I didn't really mean it," sobbed Richard. "It was a fib."

Richard dug and dug and dug all the afternoon, but he never found the place where the coins were buried.

And from that day to this, Richard never told anyone another little lie, least of all to his sister Joanna, who believed every word he said.

As for Joanna, she waited a whole year for a golden money tree to grow and drop gold coins from its branches. It did not happen, of course, but by that time she was a year older, and a much wiser little girl.

The Dream Fairy

1. Minna was a young and pretty girl, who lived all alone in one small room. She was very poor and she had to earn her living by sewing and mending clothes. When there was no mending to be done, Minna would make the most beautiful dresses, which she would take to the village to sell. All day, Minna had to work very hard. One day, one of the dream fairies saw her at her work.

2. "Poor girl, I cannot make her life any easier," sighed the dream fairy. "But at least I can make sure that at night she has happy dreams." That night, when Minna was asleep in bed, the dream fairy flew in at her window.

3. Hovering above the pillow, the dream fairy waved her magic wand. At once, Minna began to dream about the most handsome prince she had ever seen. The dream was so lovely, that Minna was sorry when morning came and it ended.

4. As soon as she awoke, she jumped out of bed and rushed to the window. The dream had seemed so real that she half expected to see the prince of her dreams riding towards her — but there was no one there. Sadly, Minna turned away from the window and began to dress. Then she picked up her needle and thread and sat down to her sewing, for she was making a lovely dress, fit for a queen.

5. But however hard Minna worked, she could not stop thinking about the handsome prince of her dream. She found it harder and harder to keep her mind on her work and every now and then she would gaze out of the window, hoping to see him.

6. The dream fairy, who was watching, knew that Minna was wishing for her dream to come true. She was not content just to dream about the handsome prince. The dream fairy sighed. "Alas, he was only made of dream dust," she said.

7. In the hope of taking Minna's mind off the prince, the dream fairy decided to give her lots of the most beautiful dreams, so that night she waved her wand over Minna's pillow again. This time, Minna dreamed she was sitting beside a sunlit pool, dabbling her feet in the cool water. Silvery fish swam in the pool and in the trees the birds sang very sweetly.

8. Next morning, Minna put the last stitches in the dress she was making. Then she picked it up and put it carefully over her arm and out she went — but she did not go to the village, to try to sell the dress. Instead she set off towards the great green forest. "At least I can make one of my dreams come true," she said to herself. "I shall search for a pool like the one in my dream."

9. Now in another part of the forest a handsome prince was hunting and he had just stopped for a rest. He looked very much like the prince whom Minna had seen in her dream.

10. The dream fairy, who happened to pass by just then, noticed this and she had a sudden idea. With a wave of her wand she made the prince dream of Minna, sitting beside the pool in the forest.

11. As quickly as it had come, the prince's dream vanished, but suddenly he remembered that he had seen just such a pool in another part of the forest. At once, the prince leapt on to his horse and rode off in search of it. He hoped that there he would find the girl he had been dreaming about, for he wanted to meet her again. The dream fairy saw this and smiled happily to herself.

12. When the prince reached the pool in the forest, he saw Minna there. She looked exactly as he had seen her in his dream. The prince was delighted and rode swiftly towards her.

13. Minna was just as delighted to see her handsome prince and they greeted each other as though they had known each other for a long time. Minna told the prince about her dream.

14. Then the prince told Minna how he had dreamed about her and the pool in the forest. "It must be magic," he said. "But I am very pleased it happened. Now I shall take you back to my palace, to meet my mother, the queen." With that, the prince put Minna on to his horse and they set off through the forest, until at last the prince's palace appeared in the distance.

15. The queen was delighted when she saw Minna and thought she was the most charming girl she had ever seen. "What fine needlework," she said, when she saw the dress Minna had made.

16. Of course, the prince had fallen in love with Minna and he wished to marry her at once. The queen was very happy with her son's choice, for she too loved Minna's sweetness and beauty.

17. As for Minna, she had never been so happy in her life as the day when she married her handsome prince. One of the guests at the wedding, though nobody saw her, was the delighted dream fairy.

Sit under my umbrella

Sit under my umbrella and talk to me.
The rain will softly drench the apple-tree.
We'll talk about giant forests and pygmy-men,
And we'll stop and peep out at the world, just now and then.

Sit under my umbrella and talk to me.
The rain will softly drench the apple-tree.
We'll talk about ships and storms and ghostly fish,
And a shark who eats his food from a golden dish!

Sit under my umbrella and have some tea!
The rain will softly drench the apple-tree.
We'll play at 'House' and chat about Uncle Joe,
And I'll tell you a fairy story, before you go.

Sit under my umbrella and talk to me.
The rain will softly drench the apple-tree.
We'll look for centipedes, big worms and snails,
And watch the birds come down — and count their tails!

The MAGICIAN'S Apprentice

Once, long ago, a youth named Hans, the youngest son of a poor woodcutter, set out to seek his fortune, with only a crust of bread, a flask of water and his own clever wits to help him.

Many offered the boy employment, for he was tall and strong and had a merry smile and a witty tongue, but he refused them all. Then, just as dusk fell, Hans met a magician who asked him to become his apprentice and learn all his magic spells from him.

"Now that is a job I would truly enjoy!" cried Hans eagerly. "Lead on, magician, I am willing to start right away."

So the magician took Hans away to his enchanted castle, at the top of which was a mysterious turret-tower where the magician cast all his spells.

But gradually it dawned on Hans that all the magician really wanted was a servant to dust and clean the castle. Hans was only allowed in the tower on one day a week, and then he was ordered merely to sweep the floor and dust the books.

If the magician found him even opening one of the heavy black spellbooks he flew into a terrible rage and threatened to turn Hans into a toad or a beetle.

But Hans was a clever young man and he was determined to gain the magic knowledge that the magician had promised to teach him.

So he awaited his chance and one day was able to steal the key to the tower. He quickly made an impression of the key with wax and returned it to the magician before his master realised that it was missing.

With the wax key Hans was able to make a steel key, and each night when the magician was asleep, he would steal softly up to the tower and start to read the spellbooks.

Soon he knew almost as much about magic as his master.

But one day the magician awoke and found Hans reading his books in the tower.

"So, thou miserable youth, thou wouldst discover my secrets," hissed the magician in rage. "For that you shall be punished."

He seized his magic wand but, before he could utter one word, Hans himself had uttered a magic incantation and in a trice had transformed himself into a white dove.

Swiftly he flew out of the open window. The he realised to his horror, that the magician, in the form of a fierce falcon, was quickly gaining upon him.

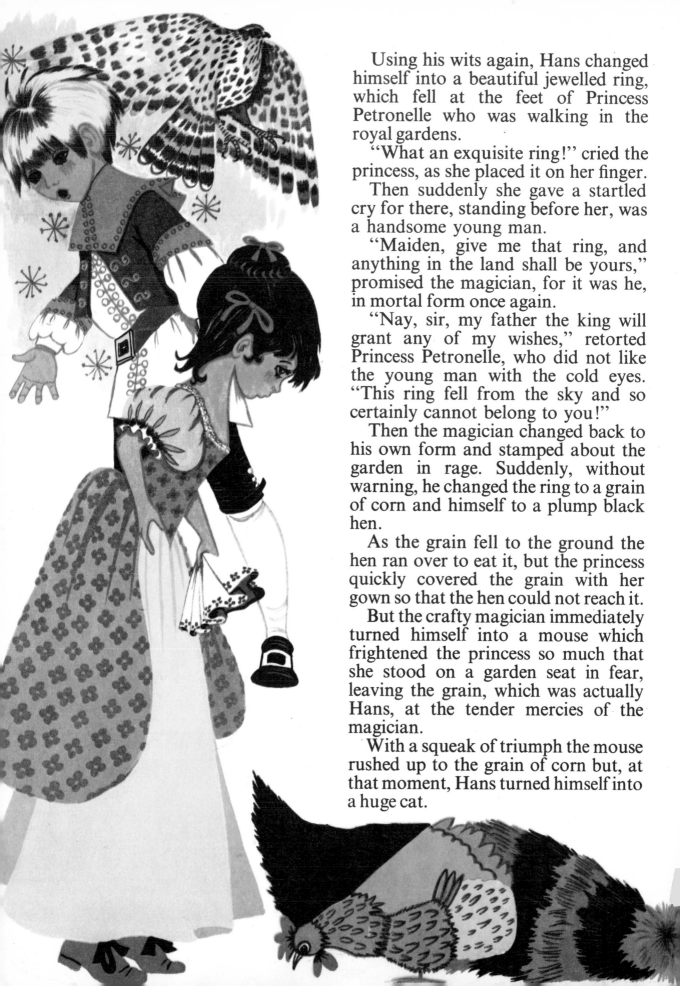

Using his wits again, Hans changed himself into a beautiful jewelled ring, which fell at the feet of Princess Petronelle who was walking in the royal gardens.

"What an exquisite ring!" cried the princess, as she placed it on her finger.

Then suddenly she gave a startled cry for there, standing before her, was a handsome young man.

"Maiden, give me that ring, and anything in the land shall be yours," promised the magician, for it was he, in mortal form once again.

"Nay, sir, my father the king will grant any of my wishes," retorted Princess Petronelle, who did not like the young man with the cold eyes. "This ring fell from the sky and so certainly cannot belong to you!"

Then the magician changed back to his own form and stamped about the garden in rage. Suddenly, without warning, he changed the ring to a grain of corn and himself to a plump black hen.

As the grain fell to the ground the hen ran over to eat it, but the princess quickly covered the grain with her gown so that the hen could not reach it.

But the crafty magician immediately turned himself into a mouse which frightened the princess so much that she stood on a garden seat in fear, leaving the grain, which was actually Hans, at the tender mercies of the magician.

With a squeak of triumph the mouse rushed up to the grain of corn but, at that moment, Hans turned himself into a huge cat.

A moment later the mouse—and, of course, the magician—was no more, and Hans was safe to restore himself to his own form.

He quickly told the astonished princess about his apprenticeship with the magician and she took him to see her father, the king.

The king decided that it would be a very good idea to have a clever magician for his son-in-law, and he asked Hans and the princess if they would like to marry.

Both the young people were delighted at this suggestion, for Princess Petronelle had fallen instantly in love with Hans, and he, in turn, realised that as well as being as beautiful as the dawn, she had a kind heart.

So Hans and his princess were married, and for many years Hans delighted and amazed the court with his many magical tricks – but he never turned himself into a mouse, because, of course, the princess would have squealed with fright!

And later, when two beautiful children were born to them, the little prince and princess loved to hear their father tell of the days when he worked as a magician's apprentice and learnt to make magic.

THE ELVES AND THE SHOEMAKER

But next morning when he went into his workshop the shoemaker found that the shoes were already beautifully sewn. Puzzled, but very pleased, he called to his wife to see them. "They are the finest shoes I have ever seen!" cried Sarah.

Once, long ago, there lived a poor shoemaker who worked hard and long, but his fortunes never prospered. At last he had only enough leather to make just one more pair of shoes. Late that evening Thomas cut out the leather by candlelight, and left it on his workbench ready to start work in the morning. Then, sadly, he and his wife went off to bed.

The shoemaker put the shoes in the centre of his window, where they were seen by the Mayor. He came in and bought them for five golden pieces. With the money, Thomas bought more leather, and cut it out and left it once more on his workbench.

Next morning two more exquisite pairs of shoes were ready and waiting to be sold. "These are fit for a nobleman!" cried Thomas, as he admired the neat stitching and delicate embroidery.

"You are right, husband," replied Sarah, as a fine carriage stopped outside the shop. In came a wealthy lord and he bought the shoes for himself and his son.

Each evening Thomas cut out the leather for the shoes, and every morning several pairs of shoes were ready to be sold. News of the wonderful shoes travelled near and far, and people flocked to the shoemaker's shop to buy his lovely shoes. Soon Thomas and his wife grew rich, and they were very happy with their good fortune.

But the shoemaker and his wife grew curious about their secret helpers, and one night, as Christmas drew near, they decided to stay up and see what would happen. So, leaving a candle burning on the bench, they hid behind a curtain.

As the clock struck midnight, in through the half-open window danced two little elves.

Quickly the two little elves settled down to work, and the shoemaker and his wife watched in amazement as the needles flew in and out and pair after pair of shoes was finished.

Then, their work completed, the elves left as silently as they had appeared.

So for the next few days the shoemaker and his wife were very busy making clothes and shoes for the elves. Sarah made each little fellow a vest, shirt, jerkin and trousers, a pair of stockings and a cap, and Thomas made two pair of gay red boots.

Next morning, when they sat down at breakfast, Sarah said to her husband: "Did you see how poorly clad those two dear little creatures were, Thomas? They have been so good to us that I feel I must repay their kindness. I shall make them some new clothes." "Then I shall make them each a fine pair of boots," replied Thomas.

Then, when all was ready, Thomas and Sarah put the clothes on the workbench, and they hid behind the curtain to watch the elves.

When they saw the clothes the elves were really delighted.

The elves put on the clothes, and laughing and chattering happily to each other, they admired themselves in the mirror. One seized a silver thimble and put it on his head for a hat; but when he saw the gay cap that Sarah had made for him he put that on instead.

Behind the curtain Thomas and Sarah gazed at each other happily, glad that their gifts had been so well received.

Suddenly, the two little elves leapt upon the table and began to sing a little song:

"Now, dear friends, we bid farewell,
For you must know, for oft folk tell,
How fairies given gifts must flee away,
And so, alas, no longer can we stay."

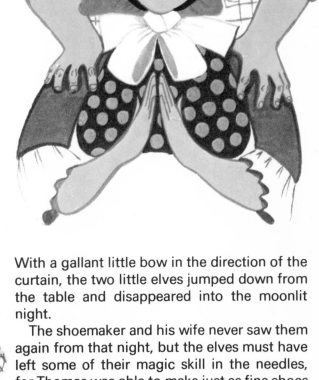

With a gallant little bow in the direction of the curtain, the two little elves jumped down from the table and disappeared into the moonlit night.

The shoemaker and his wife never saw them again from that night, but the elves must have left some of their magic skill in the needles, for Thomas was able to make just as fine shoes as ever. His shop was never empty of customers and he and his wife lived happily together in wealth and comfort, thanks to the help of the two little elves.

NESTOR NEWS, The Weatherman of Windy Willows

Do you know what a weathervane is? You will probably see one on your church spire, and it shows the direction the wind is blowing.

Your weathervane has probably been made by skilled craftsmen, but down in Windy Willows they have a very special weathervane.

It perches on top of a tall twisty chimney of the cottage belonging to Nestor News . . . and this is the story of Nestor's weathervane and how he got his name.

Nestor was once just called Nestor, but that was before the folk of Windy Willows started to have trouble with their weather.

It all started when Clarence Cuckoo took offence. You see, he heard Dame Dumpling call him a lazy bird for not building a nest of his own, and putting his wife's eggs into the nests of other birds for them to hatch them out.

"I've been too busy telling everyone that spring has arrived," Clarence called crossly. "And all you can do is call me lazy. Very well, folk of Windy Willows, if that's how you reward me, I shan't bother calling here again.

And he didn't! And what made matters worse was that Clarence told all his friends about the quarrel he had with the Windy Willows folk and as a result many strange things happened!

The winds, north, south, east and

they made poor Mr. Cringle feel so warm that his face was as hot as fire when he arrived at Moppet Cottage.

One by one, other folk in the village complained of the tricks the winds played on them. A complete summer picnic was spoilt because the west wind refused to come and sent the cold north wind instead; but when the north wind was needed to freeze the ice on the pond, the south wind came, and once again the children's fun was spoilt.

At last Nestor, who was a very

west, played tricks in Windy Willows. The north and east winds, which everyone knows are cold and chilly, began to blow soft and warm.

Dame Dumpling had just sat out in her swinging hammock in the garden when the north wind showed himself in his true colours, and blew so hard and cold that poor Dame Dumpling caught a chill and had to stay in bed for a week.

Thinking it was to be a cold, rainy day, old Mr. Cringle over at the other side of Windy Willows put on his raincoat and thick scarf, his wellingtons and warm gloves before setting off to meet his old friend Mistress Moppet.

But scarcely had he got his umbrella up before the mischievous south wind, who had been playing another naughty trick, told his friend the sun to come out from behind the clouds, and together

small man with a very large kind heart, decided that something must be done about the winds' behaviour.

He had a very high twisty chimney, as I have told you, and because he was so small he could climb right to the top of the chimney and actually hear what the winds were saying!

So he built a weathervane in the shape of a cock which sat on four points, showing the north, south, east and west, and when he heard which wind was to blow that day, he turned his weathervane round slowly by pushing it with a tall stick. Sometimes it got rather hot in the chimney, and then Nestor fanned

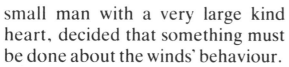

himself with a little fan to keep himself cool.

When the rest of the folk in Windy Willows realised what Nestor was doing for them they were very grateful.

"Nestor, we saw your weathervane pointing south, so we are going on our country ramble today," said Miss Addie, the village schoolteacher.

"Nestor, we have cancelled our carnival and we are going to hold it on the first day you tell us the weather will be fine!" cried Dame Dimple a few days later. "Really, it is wonderful to have someone to give us the correct weather news every day. Goodness, that's what we should call you ... Nestor News!"

"Well, it is made up of the first letters of north, south, east and west!" laughed Nestor, "so I suppose it is a good name for me. But you will be pleased to know that Dame Nature has been scolding Clarence Cuckoo and the winds for being so naughty, and they have promised to behave in future. Clarence has promised to come calling early next spring, and the winds are going to blow *exactly* as they should!"

"Does that mean you will be giving up your job?" asked Dame Dimple. "I shall be sorry if you do. I look for your weathervane sign each morning."

"Goodness, no, I like doing the job too much," replied Nestor

firmly. "And really, the winds are now great friends of mine, so they will just tell me which one of them will be blowing and I shall let you all know."

"Oh, I am glad," smiled Dame Dimple, and as she went on her way, she sang a little song:

"Up by the chimney there is a small man,
Who holds in his hand a stick and a fan;
When the winds rage he strikes a fierce blow,
And thus their direction tells mortals below."

THE GOOD WITCH

Witch Greeneyes is a kind old witch
Who only casts good spells.
And with her black cat, Sootytoes,
Down in the Magic Glade dwells.

She found a wand a fairy lost,
She helped a small bird to fly,
And made sure at the elves' picnic
No clouds darkened the blue sky.

She gave a kind little pixie
As a gift, a wishing hat,
Because he'd bathed the injured paw
Of Sootytoes, her pet cat.

And if you go round at midnight
To her house on Halloween,
You can join her birthday party —
'Tis the gayest ever seen.

The UGLY DUCKLING

The sun shone warmly on the fields of golden corn and green oats. In the farmyard the animals chattered loudly and near the meadow the stork was chattering in Egyptian as usual. In fact everything was as usual, except for the duck. Instead of chattering eagerly in the farmyard with her friends, she sat alone in the weeds by the pond, waiting for her chicks to hatch. But it was taking a very long time, and she was extremely tired.

At last, however, the eggs began to crack. First one pretty head and then another appeared from the eggs. "Quack, quack," the ducklings cried in squeaky voices, as they tried to look at everything in their new world at once. The mother duck looked joyfully at her brood, their plump fluffy bodies wobbling on spindly legs, and she sighed: "At last my job is done."

But it wasn't, for there, hidden in a corner lay one more egg. Dutifully the mother duck sat down to wait once more . . .

A few days later the last egg finally cracked, but instead of a fluffy duckling popping out, out stepped a very strange bird indeed. Its large body was covered with ugly feathers which were the same colour as the grey-brown mud at the edge of the pond and every time it tried to stand up on its long clumsy legs, *plonk*, it would fall down again.

The mother duck was very disappointed at this duckling's appearance, but shrugging her shoulders she gathered her brood together and shepherded them to the farmyard.

"Aah," cried the oldest duck in the farmyard, who counted herself in charge of all of them, "they are indeed beautiful children, each and every . . . . But who is that one, surely he isn't one of yours!"

The mother duck sighed sadly as the other animals gathered round to look at the ugly duckling: "It is as well that he is big and strong, for I think he will face many problems in this world," she said to herself.

It seemed as though the ugly duckling would never get any peace. Even though he was the best swimmer in the brood the other ducks would not accept him, they bit him and beat him with their wings and even his brothers and sisters were unkind to him. The hens and the mighty cockerel pecked him with their sharp beaks and even the girl who fed the poultry kicked him out of the way.

One day, he could stand it no longer: "I am so ugly that nobody likes me, I might just as well run away and hide where nobody will see me." And with that he ran across the farmyard and through the hedge . . . and then he ran and ran and ran.

At last he came to a large moor where some wild ducks lived. Exhausted, he lay down and fell asleep.

In the grey light of morning a flock of wild ducks saw the ugly duckling and they came to see who he was. At length one of them said: "You are indeed very ugly, but we will not hold that against you. You may stay with us."

A few days later, as the duckling huddled amongst the reeds, two more wild ducks flew up. "You are as ugly as the other ducks say, but we do not mind. You may fly with us to visit some very pretty geese on the next moor, if you like."

Without any more ado the two wild ducks flew into the air. Then . . . *bang*! From out of the reeds a shot was fired. Only a moment later the two proud ducks fell to the ground.

The duckling hid under his wing in terror, but he had little to fear. Even the big fierce dog, with sharp white teeth, who came splashing among the reeds, ignored him. The little duckling was so thankful. "Well, I suppose, that being ugly does have its better side," he said. "Even that big dog wouldn't eat me!"

He waited until nightfall, until all the firing had ceased, and then he ran away, far away from the moor.

Hours later the ugly duckling found a tumble-down hut where he thought he might shelter. Inside sat a woman who was very, very old and couldn't see very well — and her two pets, a cat and a hen. But the two creatures were very bossy; the cat considered himself master of the house and the hen considered herself mistress.

After only a few days in their company the duckling could stand their jeering and bossiness no longer, and so he started out on his travels once more.

Autumn came, the leaves turned brown and yellow, and then winter came too, freezing the ground hard and making the water very cold. The ugly duckling was very unhappy. Often he had to swim about all day, just to stop a small piece of his pond from freezing over completely.

But one day he saw something which cheered him up, just a little. Overhead flew the most beautiful birds he had ever seen, their snowy white necks gracefully outstretched as they flew to warmer lands.

The ugly duckling turned round and round in the water, until at last they were gone.

That night, however, it was colder than ever and eventually the duckling gave up his struggle to stop the ice freezing and lay down.

Luckily, a farmer passing by early in the morning found him, and soon he was in a warm kitchen. Once he was revived, the farmer's children tried to play with him, but all they did was to frighten him. Into the milk pail he flew, sending the milk all over the floor and then, frightened by the shouts and screams, he went straight into the butter barrel, and then into the meal barrel. What a sight he looked!

Once more the ugly duckling found himself on the icy moors. But eventually, after many hard-ships, he saw the first signs of spring. Larks sang, fresh, green buds appeared on the trees, and even his wings felt a little stronger, as he flew farther and farther and farther.

The garden in which he landed was beautiful. Sunlight touched the fresh green grass, apple blossom filled the trees and the air was filled with the sweet smell of lilac. In one part of the garden ran a canal and there swam three proud swans. Suddenly the duckling felt very sad.

"All my life I have been running away. Would it not be better to be killed by these kingly birds, than to look forward to a life of misery? No longer would I need to suffer the cold winters, and the vicious kicks of poultry girls," he said. "It will all be over."

Quickly he ran into the water and swam towards the beautiful birds. Slowly they turned their heads, and then they swam towards him.

"Kill me," the duckling cried, and bowed his head low.

But what was that in the water? Yes, yes, it was his own reflection. But no longer that of an ugly grey bird, he was now a beautiful white swan.

Oh, how happy the ugly duckling was, now that he was a swan. Children came into the garden and threw bread and cake to them, and when one family came the youngest child cried: "See, there is a new one!" And the whole family came to look at him. "Yes," they agreed, "this new swan is so young and graceful. He must surely be the most beautiful one of all."

The young swan bowed his head, for he was not proud or vain. It wasn't easy to forget how taunted and unhappy he had been as a duckling, and when he lifted his head to the sky it wasn't out of pride. It was simply that he was so very happy.

THE FAIRY COACH

Drawn by four golden butterflies,
Harnessed by silver cobweb reins,
The royal coach is driven through
Fairyland's green-meadowed lanes.

The coachman is a small wee elf,
In a cap and suit of bright green,
And strong boots of gay red leather,
The finest pair you've ever seen.

Two fairy coachmen guard the rear,
Standing there, so silent and tall,
And though the coach may jog about,
Never once, do they ever fall.

While inside sits the fairy queen,
So beautiful, kind and sweet,
Smiling out so graciously
At all whom she may meet.

She's on her way to Goblin Grove,
To meet the Goblin King,
Who today invited her to hear
His Goblin choir sing.

And as he passes through her realm,
All her subjects so proudly say:
"Doesn't our royal coach look grand?"
As it speeds swiftly on its way.

The ODD JOB MEN

One fine day the five little goblins who live in the pretty pink toadstool house with a red top which is on the shores of the big lake in Goblin Land, were sitting in their garden looking out over the blue waters.

"I wish we had a little shop," said one of the little goblins, whose name was Hobbledy. He had just been to the sweet shop down in the village to buy some sweets.

"Don't be silly," said another little goblin called Hoppity. "We can't have a shop because we have not got anything to sell."

"So we haven't," agreed the first little goblin glumly. "Still," he added, "it would have been nice."

The five little goblins sat still and quiet for a moment, looking out over the water again and thinking how nice it would have been to have a nice little shop, with a nice little counter, and a nice little till that went *ping* every time you opened it to put some money in.

Suddenly a third little goblin, whose name was Hoy, jumped up.

"We could have a shop," he cried excitedly. "Only we would not sell *things*, we would sell odd jobs!"

"Sell odd jobs!" echoed the other little goblins in surprise. "What ever do you mean?"

And they looked at him anxiously to see if maybe he had been out in the sun too long and did not quite know what he was saying.

"Don't you see?" the little goblin Hoy demanded. "We could be odd job men. There is always someone in Goblin Land who wants a roof repairing, or a chair mended, or a chimney swept, or a carpet cleaned, or something painted, or lots and lots of other things. Well, we could do the jobs for them."

Now that he had explained just what he meant, the other little goblins could see that it might be a very good idea indeed.

"How will we let people know what we are doing?" they asked.

"We will have a notice board up in the garden with our names on it and 'odd job men' written underneath in big writing and then everyone who goes past will see it," the little goblin who had thought of the idea in the first place told them.

Two of the little goblins jumped up and ran to fetch a long wooden post. They were Hibbledy and Hobbledy. Two more little goblins, Hoppity and Hoy, ran to fetch a big, big piece of card to write the notice on, and the fifth little goblin, whose name was Egbert, ran to get a pot of paint, and a paint brush, and a hammer, and some nails.

When they had collected everything together they took the big piece of card, and the paint brush and the paint, and they painted their names very neatly and carefully in big letters that everyone could see.

HIBBLEDY HOBBLEDY
HOPPITY HOY AND
EGBERT

and then underneath that they wrote,
ODD JOB MEN

Then they stood back to enjoy their handiwork.

"Yes, that will do nicely," they all agreed after they had looked at it from all angles. "It will do very nicely indeed."

HIBBLEDY HOBBLEDY HOPPITY HOY AND EGBERT
ODD JOB MEN

They laid the notice carefully on the grass so that the paint could dry properly. Then they took the long wooden post that Hibbledy and Hobbledy had brought and pushed one end of it deep into the ground by the front gate so that it stood up straight and firm, and they stamped the earth in hard all round it so that it would not fall over if you leaned on it or if you bumped into it by mistake.

By the time they had finished doing that, they thought that the paint must be dry, so they went back to have a look. It *looked* dry, so Egbert touched it very gently with one finger. Yes, it *was* dry. They carried it down to the gate.

Hibbledy, Hobbledy, Hoppity and Hoy lifted Egbert up onto their shoulders so that he could reach the top of the wooden post, and then they handed him one hammer and two nails, and he tap, tap, tapped the notice board into place.

When they had lowered Egbert to the ground again they stepped back to take another look at their handiwork now that it was finished.

They looked at it from the front, and then they looked at it from one side, and then from the other side, and then they went out through the gate and looked at it from the road, and then they smiled proudly at each other.

Yes, it really did look businesslike.

The five little goblins trooped indoors to wait, with their noses pressed to the window, for their first customer.

They did not have long to wait either, because very soon Old Grandpa

Grumbletoes came along the road. At first he walked right past the notice board as if he had not seen it, then he stopped suddenly and came back to read it.

The five goblins watched anxiously from their window as Old Grandpa Grumbletoes read it once, then scratched his nose, then read it again and took off his funny tall hat and scratched his shiny bald head, and then read the notice a third time.

At last he seemed to have made up his mind. He opened the gate and went up the path to the toadstool house and knocked on the little door knocker.

Hibbledy, Hobbledy, Hoppity, and Hoy, and Egbert, rushed to open the door, and Old Grandpa Grumbletoes blinked in surprise as five pairs of eyes gazed eagerly at him, and five voices chorused, "Can we help you?"

"Well," said Old Grandpa Grumbletoes, trying not to laugh. "There is something I want doing. There seems to be something stuck in my chimney. Every time I try to light the fire the smoke comes out all over the room and makes everything sooty, and it makes me cough and sneeze so much that I have to put the fire out again. I'm just on my way to market now," he added. "Could you have the job finished by the time I get back?"

"Oh, yes. Indeed we can," the goblins told him.

"Well, mind you tidy up after you and do not leave any mess about," warned Old Grandpa Grumbletoes as he went off down the path.

When he had gone the five little goblins hurried and scurried about. They dragged their little cart out of the shed at the bottom of the garden, then they loaded it up with all the things they thought they might need. First there was a big cloth to carry the soot in, then there were their chimney sweep's brushes and sticks, and lastly their great long ladder.

At last, when they had everything piled up on the cart, they set off for Old Grandpa Grumbletoes' cottage. The cart was so heavy that they all had to push as hard as they could to keep it moving, but at last they reached their destination. They pulled their cart into Old Grandpa Grumbletoes' pathway.

They unloaded their brushes and sticks, and the big cloth for carrying away the soot, and went into the cottage. Soon they had their brush up the chimney. They pushed and turned and pushed and turned, and the brush seemed to be going up as easily as anything until suddenly it stuck fast. The goblins pushed and poked but they just could not shift it at all.

Just then they heard a terrible commotion outside the window. Mr. Sparrow was fluttering and twittering angrily outside. He looked really annoyed.

"We had better go and see what he wants," said Hibbledy.

They opened the window and put their heads out.

"Is anything the matter?" asked Hibbledy.

Little Mr. Sparrow was spluttering with rage.

"Matter!" he squawked. "Matter! I'll say something is the matter. People should not be allowed to push other peoples' homes about."

"But we have not touched your home," said Hobbledy.

"Yes, you have," answered Mr. Sparrow indignantly. "You keep sticking things up the chimney and poking it." He stopped and glared at them. "That silly Old Grumbletoes must have sent you."

"Oh, so it's your nest that is blocking up the chimney, is it?" said Hoy. "It really is awkward for Old Grandpa Grumbletoes," he explained. "You see, while your nest is in his chimney he can't have a fire because there is nowhere for the smoke to go except back into the room. That makes everywhere sooty and dirty, and it makes Old Grandpa Grumbletoes cough and sneeze so much that he

has to put his fire out."

"Serves him right," snapped Mr. Sparrow angrily.

"Couldn't you possibly build it anywhere else?" Hoy asked.

"No, we could not," Mr. Sparrow spluttered. "We had a perfectly good place for a nest last year in Old Grumbletoes tool shed, but he chased us out and locked the door. In any case we have four little eggs in our nest now," he added.

"Just a minute," Hoy told him.

He and the four other little goblins put their heads together and whispered and muttered to each other, and then they went back to the window where Mr. Sparrow was waiting.

must be careful not to break any of our eggs."

The five little goblins went out to their cart and unloaded their big long ladder. They carried it up the path, to the cottage and propped it up against the wall. Then Egbert held the bottom of the ladder to keep it steady while Hoy climbed up to the roof to scramble up the tiles to the chimney.

Hibbledy, Hobbledy, and Hoppity ran back into the house to push the nest up the chimney with their brush.

Soon Hoy and the sparrows could hear scraping and bumping noises coming up the chimney, and Mrs. Sparrow kept squeaking, "Oh, *do* be careful."

At last Hoy could reach her.

"Stop," he called down the chimney as loudly as he could.

Hibbledy, Hobbledy, and Hoppity stopped pushing.

"Now then," said Hoy to Mrs. Sparrow. "Let me put your four little eggs in my cap and I will carry them very carefully down the ladder and put them on the grass and then you can fly down and sit on them to keep them warm until I bring the nest down to you."

Mr. and Mrs. Sparrow watched anxiously as Hoy took off his hat and carefully placed the four pretty little eggs in it.

"Oh, *do* be careful," they twittered over and over again.

Hoy held his hat very tightly as he slid down the tiles and climbed down the ladder. The two sparrows flew down to join him when he had reached the bottom, and as soon as he put the eggs on to the grass Mrs. Sparrow settled herself on top of them.

After that it did not take Hoy long to bring down the nest and put it in

"Would you like to come and live in *our* wood shed?" Hoppity asked. "We could push your nest to the top of the chimney very carefully and carry it back in our little cart. You would be quite safe and happy with us, and we would put out crumbs for you every day."

Mr. Sparrow held his head on one side, and then he held it on the other side.

"I'll have to see what Mrs. Sparrow thinks," he said at last, and he flitted up to the roof to talk to his wife. Soon he came back down again, looking very pleased.

"We think that your idea is a very good one," he told them. "But you the cart. Then, with the Sparrow family safely in their home again, the five little goblins pushed their cart back to the tool shed in their own garden.

Inside the tool shed there was a big flower pot standing on the shelf. Mr. and Mrs. Sparrow decided that it was just the place for their nest. The five little goblins very gently put them inside it.

The Sparrows were very pleased with their new home. Really it was *much* better than a sooty old chimney.

Hibbledy, Hobbledy, Hoppity, Hoy, and Egbert, rushed back to Old Grandpa Grumbletoes' cottage to finish sweeping the chimney. They swept it until there was no soot left in it at all, and then they cleaned up the fireplace, packed their ladder

and brushes and things in the cart, and started for home.

On the way they met Old Grandpa Grumbletoes coming back from market.

"Have you finished already?" he asked in surprise.

The five little goblins nodded.

"And have you left everywhere clean and tidy?" he asked next.

The five little goblins told him that they had indeed left everywhere beautifully clean.

Old Grandpa Grumbletoes put his hand in his pocket and pulled out five brand new shiny silver shillings.

"Here you are," he said. And he gave one to each of the little goblins.

They thanked him very much and hurried home, tired but happy, for tea.

They decided that they were going to enjoy being odd job men very much indeed.

ISOBEL CHAFFINCH

When she was very, very young
  and found that she had wings,
She also found about the world,
  a lot of other things.
When once she flew away alone,
  delighted to be free,
She met an awful white-pawed cat
  that chased her up a tree.
She ran and flew, and flew and ran –
  her heart was beating fast
She wondered if her running powers,
  and flying powers would last,
The cat was *the* most frightful cat
  that she had ever seen,
And what was worse, its almond eyes,
  were very, very green.

Ever since the family
  came to live in Cherry Glade,
The youngest chaffinch, Isobel,
  was very much afraid.
She was afraid to leave her nest,
  and fly into the sky;
And if you think it rather odd,
  this is the reason why.

Poor Isobel was quite distraught,
  and when she reached her nest,
She vowed she'd never try again
  to fly out like the rest;
She vowed she'd never leave again
  the pink-flowered cherry tree –
Because of this most awful cat
  she did not want to see.

117

She'd met with barking dogs
   that were much bigger than a cat,
She's even met some Jersey cows,
   but THIS was worse than that!
Because this cat had got a look
   that frightened Isobel –
And what is more, she had got claws
   that frightened her as well;
When, from her nest she heard "Mee-ow"
   or even just a purr –
It was enough to scare
   the very living out of her.

One day her mother had to make
   a call on Mrs. Crow,
She brushed the wings of Isobel,
   and asked her would she go.
But Isobel was too afraid,
   although she wanted to,
And said "I'll stay at home,
   I do not want to go with you!"

The other chaffinch children
   all got ready to depart,
They had their feathers brushed,
   to make them look especially smart.
Their mother touched a buttercup
   to brighten up her beak,
And powdered with a dandelion,
   her eyebrows and her cheek.
She clutched her charges by the wings,
   and flew to Mrs. Crow,
While Isobel just sat and sulked,
   because she could not go.

For hours and hours, it seemed to her,
  she walked around her nest.
She wished that she was at a party,
  playing like the rest –
She wished that she was eating nuts
  cut up in little squares,
Or drinking rain from acorn cups
  that Mrs. Crow prepares.
She wished that she was hopping round
  and playing hide-and-seek,
Or playing other games
  like passing worms from beak to beak.

Instead of this,
  poor Isobel was sitting all alone,
She whistled for a while
  and then, at length, began to moan.
I think, thought she,
  that in this tree, I will be safe and sound,
As long as I don't fly away,
  or drop upon the ground

And so she hopped along the branch
  and sang a little song,
Because she thought that she was safe,
  but what she thought was wrong!
For just behind poor Isobel,
  and right beside her wing
A purring sound began –
  she turned, to face the awful thing . . .

That great big cat with glowing eyes,
  those awful snow-white paws!
That horrid tail that waved about,
  those terrifying claws!
A paw reached out to touch her head –
  she pulled herself away.
She flew in terror to the sky,
  her wings in disarray.
"Meeow, Meeow" that awful sound
  was all that she could hear –
And was it fate that made a dog –
  a terrier – appear?

The cat, distracted by the bark,
  rushed wildly from the tree,
And Isobel looked down and felt, at last,
  that she was free . . .
She dropped exhausted on a branch,
  and perched completely still
She watched the terrier give chase,
  the cat fly up the hill.

The pattering of paws was like
  the thunder she had heard –
A year before
  when she was just a very tiny bird.
She watched
  and she was really quite excited when she saw –
The cat get tired,
  the terrier was winning by a paw!

He barked. The cat *meeowed.*
  He turned and knocked her on the ground.
And soon a lot of other dogs arrived
  and they all gathered round.
They ran around the frightened cat;
  who spat and cried in vain.
They chased her up an almond tree,
  and chased her down again.

The cat was so exhausted
  that she could not even purr –
And Isobel was hoping
  she had seen the end of her.
And this was true –
  because no cat would dare to re-appear –
Who has been chased and thrown about,
  and bitten on the ear!

LITTLE TOMMY TITTLEMOUSE

THE STORY BEHIND THE RHYME

One warm autumn morning Tommy Tittlemouse was walking through the Whispering Woods which led into Nursery Rhyme Land.

Suddenly he spied Squeak Squirrel adding nuts to a pile he had already collected to hide away before he went to sleep for the winter.

Naughty Tommy gave a chuckle and, before poor Squeak could stop him, Tommy kicked over the pile of nuts, sending them high in the air.

"Oh, you wicked boy!" sobbed Squeak. "Now I shall have to start looking for more nuts all over again. You are horrid, Tommy! You are always playing nasty tricks on people smaller than yourself. One day you will be sorry."

But Tommy only laughed as he went on his way.

He had not gone very far when he saw Baby Bunting playing beneath a tree. In the little boy's hand was a stick of barley sugar.

Making quite sure that Father

Bunting was not anywhere near, Tommy snatched the sweet from Baby's hand, and ran off, laughing, as the little boy started to cry.

Suddenly, in a clearing in the wood, Tommy saw Polly Flinders and Molly Muffet playing with their dolls. The girls had been having a picnic, and Tommy's sharp eyes spied two cups of lemonade lying on the grass.

"I'll have one of those," he said rudely, without waiting to be asked.

But as he tried to pick one up, Molly tried to stop him and, in a temper, Tommy emptied the cup of lemonade all over Molly's dress.

"Oh, you are horrid!" cried Polly, as she tried to dry her friend's dress with her handkerchief. "Now Mistress Muffet will scold Molly for spoiling her new dress, and it wasn't her fault."

"Well, *you* are always spoiling your dresses by sitting amongst the cinders," laughed Tommy rudely. "I heard Tommy Tucker singing about it only this morning."

"Yes, but it was only because I was so cold," retorted Polly angrily. "*You* did that on purpose, Tommy, and deserve to be punished."

"And so he shall be, my dear," said a stern voice behind the children. "I have been watching you all morning, Tommy Tittlemouse, playing nasty tricks on everyone. Now it will be your turn to see how you like being small and unable to defend yourself."

"It's the Wise Woman of Whispering Woods," explained Polly softly to Molly. "People say that she has magic powers and that she rewards the good but punishes the bad."

The Wise Woman gazed sternly at Tommy, but he rudely pulled a face at her and cried: "I'm not afraid of you, Old Woman!"

"Then let us see if you are afraid of being small!" cried the Wise Woman, as from her cloak she pulled a small phial.

Before Tommy realised what was happening, the Wise Woman sprinkled a little of the silver liquid it contained on Tommy's head, crying as she did so:

> *"No longer tall*
> *This boy shall be,*
> *Until he learns*
> *To act kindly!"*

And, in a trice, before the girls' astonished eyes, Tommy shrank until he was scarcely two inches tall.

"Oh, what have you done to me?" he wept. "What shall I do?"

"You must learn to be kind," replied the Wise Woman. "Oh, look out, Tommy, here comes Ronnie Rabbit. You chased him down a burrow last week, now it is Ronnie's turn to chase you!"

"Oh dear, I do hope Tommy doesn't get hurt," cried Molly, who was a very kind-hearted little girl.

"Ronnie will only give him a fright," laughed the Wise Woman. "Don't you worry about Master Tommy, my dear. It is time that he was taught a lesson."

Meanwhile poor Tommy ran on and on, trying to outpace Ronnie. The tall grass pricked him and once, eager to see how far behind Ronnie was, he stumbled and fell into a bed of nettles.

"I'm stung, I'm stung!" he sobbed as, forcing his tired legs on, he finally crept under a bluebell and lay there.

Tommy sighed with relief as Ronnie ran past, but a moment later he gave a sharp cry of pain as he felt a stone hit his leg.

Looking up he realised that it was Squeak Squirrel pelting him with nuts.

"Oh, please stop!" begged Tommy sadly. "If you do, I will help you to collect as many nuts as I knocked over."

"Very well," replied Squeak with a grin. "You can start right away."

Poor Tommy found that each nut weighed as much as a sack of potatoes, and when he had finished he felt quite worn out.

"I'm so tired and hungry," he cried, as he made his way home.

But there another shock awaited him. His house now seemed simply enormous! He could not reach the pantry door to get any food and he was chased round and round the kitchen floor by Tibbles his cat.

When he almost feared that Tibbles would capture him, Tommy found himself pulled into a mousehole by a friendly little mouse, who generously shared her crumbs for supper with Tommy.

"You may stay here tonight," said Tabitha Mouse with a little smile. "You will be quite safe. But I'm afraid you will have to go out and search for your own breakfast. I have no food left. The boy who lives here always keeps the pantry door locked."

Tommy felt himself blushing at the little mouse's words, and he resolved always to put some food near her hole in future.

"I will if only I grow tall again," he murmured as he fell asleep.

Next morning Tommy went in search of some food for Tabitha and himself.

He managed to catch two tiny fish in the ditch stream which ran along the side of Mistress Horner's house, and he managed to rescue a piece of cheese and two curls of bacon rind from her dustbin.

Tabitha Mouse was delighted with the bacon rind and the cheese, and she kindly cooked Tommy the two fish for his breakfast.

"Nobody has ever shared their cheese with me before," she said gratefully. "You *are* a kind person."

Suddenly Tommy felt most peculiar, and he saw Tabitha gazing at him in alarm. He had only just time to rush out of the hole before the last of the spell wore off.

"Hurray, I'm tall again!" he cried. "And kind too!" he added quickly.

Bending down he called softly:

"Tabitha, you will always find the pantry door unlocked from now on."

Leaving the little mouse gazing after him in amazement, Tommy rushed over to Polly's house to show her that all was well and to apologise for his bad behaviour.

From that day Tommy always tried to be kind and good, but whenever he forgot and was naughty, Tommy Tucker would sing softly in his ear:

"Little Tommy Tittlemouse
Lived in a little house.
He caught fishes
In other men's ditches!"

And Tommy would remember his meeting with the Wise Woman of Whispering Woods and try even harder to be good!

The Enchanted Deer

ONCE upon a time there lived the King of Morento, and he was very sad and unhappy because he had no children. He was always praying for a son and sought advice from anybody who wished to visit his Palace. But no advice was any good and his hopes faded away.

One day, tired of praying and listening to what other people told him, he decided to close his Palace to visitors. However, a very wise old man from a distant land happened to pass that way on his travels and not knowing that the King had changed his ideas, he knocked on the Palace door. The King in person went to open it and scowled at the sight of the old man.

"Go away," he said. "The Palace is no longer open to travellers."

"Why?" asked the wise old man. "Because I'm weary and unhappy with everything," replied the King. "I have never been blessed with children of my own and I do not wish to see anybody."

"Would you like some good advice?" said the wise old man. "Send your servants to the top of the high mountain on the border of your Kingdom to collect some blue figs which only grow there on a certain tree. Then have these blue figs cooked in some of the finest wine and give them to the Queen to eat. By that means you will have the son you pray for."

The King thought about it and decided to try it. He gave orders to the servants and they climbed the high mountain to collect a few of the rare blue figs.

The Palace cook was told how to prepare them with wine and she later presented the Queen with the dishful of delicious figs. They were soon eaten by Her Majesty — and, wonder of wonders, she later gave birth to a lovely son, whom she named Andrea.

But on the very same day, the Palace cook, who had only breathed in the smell of the cooking blue figs when she was preparing them, also gave birth to a lovely son. She called him Rolando.

Now the two little boys were just like twins. They grew up together and became very attached to each other. Rolando, the cook's son, was taught to read and write by the same Palace teacher and became as clever as Prince Andrea himself.

However, little by little the Queen began to worry about this. She was not happy to see that Andrea liked the company of Rolando better than even her own. Her jealousy grew greater and greater until one day in the Palace when Andrea was not present, she slapped Rolando in the face.

Rolando, more sad than hurt, then realised that his presence in the Palace was causing trouble between the Queen and Prince Andrea, so he decided that he must leave.

"But why are you going?" asked Andrea.

"I would like to see other parts of the world," Rolando told him.

When the moment came for the two youngsters to say goodbye to each other, Andrea asked Rolando to leave behind some sign of his friendship. This Rolando did by sticking a sword into the ground. At the spot where the sword pierced the soil a plant at once grew and a small stream of water trickled from its roots.

"Watch that stream of water very closely," Rolando told Andrea. "If you see it is clear then you will know that I am in good health. If it becomes cloudy you will know that I am in danger. If it dries up altogether, you will know that I am dead. Also, the plant will remain green while I still live, but will die if I also die."

Having said this, Rolando embraced Andrea and departed.

After many adventures he came to a faraway Kingdom where a tournament between knights on

horseback was about to take place
—and the winner would gain the
lovely daughter of the King as a
wife.

Rolando was strong and a good
horseman. He entered the tournament and defeated all his opponents
quite easily. Thus he married the
Princess and so became a Prince
himself. And he was very happy at
the court, until one day when he
thought he would go hunting.

"Don't do that," the King asked
him. "In these woods there lives
an ogre, who changes his appearance at will. Sometimes he appears
as a goat, or a lion, or a deer. He
leads hunters to his cave and there
eats them!"

Rolando was not afraid and
decided that he would go hunting
despite the King's advice. So he
went into the wood and soon he
saw a beautiful deer, which ran
away from him. Rolando gave
chase. The chase led him across a
stream and through a waterfall,
which resulted in Rolando getting
so wet that he went into a cave to
light a fire and dry his clothes.

While he was doing this, and not
knowing that he was already almost
in the clutches of the wicked ogre,
he saw the deer come to the mouth
of the cave. "Good knight, please
let me warm myself," it pleaded.

"Come right in," said Rolando.

"I daren't, because I'm frightened
of your sword," said the deer.

"In that case, I'll get rid of it,"
said Rolando and he threw his
sword away to the back of the cave.

At once the deer altered appearance and changed to the shape of
the wicked ogre! In one bound he
seized Rolando and threw him
into a ditch which he covered with
a huge stone. "I'll eat you later,
when you are fatter and I am ready

for a good supper," said the ogre.

Meanwhile, what was happening back in the Kingdom of Morento? Twice a day Andrea had been watching the little stream and the plant, and when he saw one morning that the stream had clouded and the plant looked limp and dry, he jumped on his horse and went in search of Rolando.

At length he came to the other Kingdom and found everyone in a state of great sadness, believing Rolando to be dead.

Now, as you remember, Andrea and Rolando were rather like twins. When she saw Andrea, the Princess flung her arms around his neck and begged him to go into the wood in search of her missing husband. But she gave him good warning of the ogre and the enchanted deer.

"Do not be deceived by its sweet appearance and pleadings," she told him. "Remember, always, that it is really the wicked ogre in disguise!"

Thus forewarned, Andrea went into the woods with a strong hunting dog. They soon met the enchanted deer which led them a chase across the stream and through the waterfall. Andrea behaved exactly as Rolando had done by going into the cave to light a fire and dry his clothes.

And, as before, the enchanted deer appeared, and asked if it could come nearer to warm itself by the fire.

"Certainly," replied Andrea.

"But I am afraid of your dog," said the deer.

"You do well to be afraid, ogre in disguise!" shouted Andrea, and he let the hunting dog loose. With a howl of terror the ogre turned to run, but the fleet footed dog soon captured him.

Then Andrea turned to look round for Rolando. Hearing a cry from the ditch near the cave, he rolled away the big stone and there found his lost friend.

The two young men were overjoyed to see each other again. Delightedly they returned to the Kingdom and there was great happiness when Prince Rolando greeted his Princess wife.

So the region was forever rid of its ogre and no one saw the enchanted deer again. As for Rolando, he gave Andrea a note to take back to the Kingdom of Morento, asking his mother to join him.

His mother did so . . . but not any more as a Palace cook.

Hans and the Hare

1. Young Hans, who lived in a Dutch town, had fallen madly in love with Gretchen, the daughter of a wealthy merchant. But Hans could not be happy because the family kept him away.

2. The father, mother and two brothers stood guard outside the house and would not let him in to see Gretchen. And she, poor girl, was locked in a room inside and not allowed to go out and meet Hans.

3. Hans walked sadly away from the rich merchant's home, thinking how awful and unhappy life could be. Then suddenly his thoughts were broken into by a big hare, which came racing along the road and jumped into his arms. "Save me," it said.

4. "There is a fox after me, good sir, and the last thing in the world I wish for is to be a fox's dinner." Hans felt sorry for the hare and when the fox came along that way he shouted at it and beat it off with a thick stick.

5. When the fox had gone, Hans told the hare about his own troubles. "You must be bolder, Hans," the hare told him. "You were bold enough to rescue me, so have courage and speak to her father."

6. So, encouraged by the hare, Hans took a deep breath and marched to the house of the rich merchant. "Very well then," laughed Gretchen's father. "If you can reach my daughter, you can have her."

7. Now this was easier said than done. The father stood guard at one door of the house and the mother stood guard at another. Both looked very sternly at Hans, as if daring him to step nearer, and try to force his way past them.

8. "Come along, what are you waiting for, young fellow?" chuckled the father. "You have only to walk in and reach my daughter, you know." Hans thought he would try another way into the house, for he could not pass the parents.

9. He hurried round to the side, but there he saw the two brothers standing guard outside Gretchen's window. And she, poor girl, was locked in. Hans was very puzzled and unhappy about this.

10. But the cunning hare came along to take a hand in the game and scampered past the mother, who shouted: "A fine fat hare for supper!" And picking up her skirts she started to chase it.

11. Her excited cries brought father on to the scene. "What is it, wife?" he asked. "What are you running for?" "I am after a fine big hare," she panted in reply. "It will do for our supper if we can catch it, so don't stop me."

12. "Stop you? Why, that's the very last thing I would do, my good woman," cried the father. "I'm very fond of a well-cooked hare for supper, so I'll join you and help you to catch it." So the merchant followed along behind his wife.

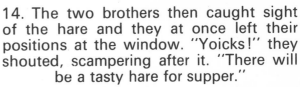

13. Now that hare was travelling very fast and neither the father nor the mother could keep up with it. "Help us," they shouted to the two brothers on guard outside Gretchen's window.

14. The two brothers then caught sight of the hare and they at once left their positions at the window. "Yoicks!" they shouted, scampering after it. "There will be a tasty hare for supper."

15. But the hare led them such a chase round and round the house that all four of them could keep it up no longer. Feeling dizzy, they sank exhausted to the ground—just as the hare wanted. "All clear now, Hans!" he called out.

16. That was how Hans was able to walk into the house and take the fair hand of the lovely Gretchen. "I have got you," he said, "so your father will not stop our marriage." And it turned out like that—thanks to the hare.

The Magic Red Fish

Pedro was a fisherman who lived in Spain. He was very poor and he and his wife had a small wooden hut close to the seashore. It was not much of a place to live in, and Pedro's wife grumbled about it all the time.

"What a terrible place we have to live in," she complained. "You must catch more fish to sell in the market. One day, perhaps, we will be able to move from this wooden hut to a nice cottage made of stone. I'm sure we could do it, if you were not so lazy."

Pedro sighed. He was not lazy at all. The truth of the matter was that there never seemed to be many fish to catch. From early morning until late at night, he cast his net into the sea, until his arms ached.

One day, however, when his wife had been complaining even more bitterly than usual, Pedro was overjoyed to feel something in his net.

It was a big fish—a big red fish, in fact. Pedro was about to seize it, when to his great surprise, the red fish spoke to him. "Please spare me, fisherman

Pedro," it said. "If you let me go, I promise that in return I will give you a great reward, for I am a magic red fish."

Pedro hesitated. He did not want to give up his splendid catch, but the red fish pleaded so much to be set free that he tipped it out of the net and let it drop back into the sea.

"Thank you, Pedro," called the fish, as it swam out of sight. "Do not forget. If you need anything, just call me."

Thoughtfully, Pedro returned to his home to tell his wife about the strange happening. When he got to the part about the red fish promising him a reward, his wife shouted at him. "You silly man," she shrieked. "Go back to the seashore at once and ask the fish for a cottage of stone, instead of this miserable wooden hut."

So Pedro went back and called to the red fish. "It is not a lot to wish for," it told him. "Return home and you will see some of my magic."

Hurrying back home, Pedro was amazed and delighted to see his wife sitting at the door of a beautiful stone cottage.

She seemed pleased, but it did not last. After a few days, she was grumbling again. "This is not really enough," she sniffed in a proud manner. "What I wanted was a castle to live in, and a host of servants to wait upon me. Go at once to the red fish and tell it what I say."

Sad to see that his wife was so greedy, poor Pedro returned to the seashore. He called to the red fish and explained that his wife was not satisfied and wanted a splendid castle.

"Your wish shall be granted," said the fish, with a wave of one of its fins. "Now return home and see what has happened."

When Pedro got back, he just stood

and stared in wonder and surprise. There was his wife, seated at a table in a splendid castle garden, being handed tea and cakes by two servants.

"I shall have no more of her complaints now," thought Pedro.

But, alas, he was mistaken. By next day even, his wife was tired of the castle and made Pedro go to the magic red fish with a demand that she be made a Queen in a Royal Palace.

"Very well," agreed the fish. "It shall be done."

On returning, Pedro found in place of the castle a beautiful Royal Palace. In a great hall he found his wife sitting on a golden throne like a Queen.

"Ah, at last she will be very happy," thought the fisherman, but he was wrong.

By tea-time, the discontented wife was grumbling again. "I don't want to be just a Queen," she snapped. "I want to be the Empress of the whole world!"

So Pedro had to go and call the fish once more and tell it that his wife wanted to be the Empress of the world.

"Very well," said the fish. "Her wish will be granted."

This time, when he went back, Pedro was astounded to see an even bigger palace, built of shining white marble, with a roof of solid gold. And in one of the great rooms, the poor fisherman found his wife sitting on a huge golden throne, wearing a dress covered with diamonds and pearls. She seemed highly pleased.

But on the following morning when the new Empress of the world looked out of the palace window, she started to grumble.

"What a dreadful day," she said. "The sky is full of ugly black clouds and it makes me feel so miserable. Go to the fish at once and tell it that I want to be the most important person in Heaven, so that I can make the sun shine whenever I like."

As she spoke, a wild storm broke out. Rain and sleet came slashing down from a sky black with thunderclouds. The trees bent under the force of a wild, howling gale.

Pedro made his way to the seashore, very scared by the thunder and lightning. He shouted to the fish and when it came out of the angry sea, he told it his wife's latest wish.

"Go home and you will find that she has been given her proper reward for wishing such a thing," said the Magic Red Fish, and with a swish of its tail it turned and headed far out to sea.

Pedro went slowly back home. The palace had disappeared. His wife, dressed in her tattered clothes, was sitting on a stone in front of their old wooden hut.

She was back where she had started, and all because of her greed. But at least the magic of the red fish had done Pedro a great deal of good, for, from that day onwards, his wife did not grumble again.

SAM'S SECRET

Sam Squirrel sat in the doorway of his house in the oak tree, enjoying his supper of nuts and berries, and listening to the peaceful evening noises in the wood. He was peeling his last juicy hazelnut when a most unfortunate thing happened. A pair of chattering magpies perched on a bough nearby and, quite by accident, he heard all that they said. Naturally he would never have listened to a private conversation, but he was so upset by their talk that he just could not move.

"It's a pity about poor old Sam," one magpie began.

"He used to be such good company – now he's no fun at all."

The second magpie clicked his beak in agreement.

"He thinks we don't notice," he remarked. "But we all know that he has lost his nerve. Remember how he used to leap from tree to tree, and run far out on the branches and chat to us? Now he creeps up and down the tree trunk, but never plays in the branches. He's scared of slipping."

Then the first magpie said, "I'm

Sadly he crept into bed, curled his beautiful red tail over his face, and thought seriously about moving house. Perhaps the rabbit family in the roots of his oak would give him a room. Now that his friends knew his secret there was no point in trying to hide it any longer.

Just about the time that Sam was drifting into an unhappy sleep, the New Moon sailed up into the sky. He was very new and very frisky. In no time at all, he was playing hide-and-seek with a group of little clouds. Carelessly he skipped over the sky, not bothering to look where he was going. And where he went was straight into the boughs of Sam's oak tree. One of his silver horns caught in a cluster of twigs, and he was held fast.

Hearing his cries, the woodland creatures dashed to the rescue. The birds tugged with beak and claw at the branch that held him. Some of them even jumped on top of him and tried to rock him free until he complained crossly that they were too heavy. At this, the Owl – in a temper because his hunting had been disturbed – called him a giddy, ungrateful youngster. And the poor Moon cried harder than ever.

afraid he has become such a coward that he seems more like a rabbit than a squirrel."

Hidden in his doorway, poor Sam sat with his head in his paws. It was all true. He was afraid. He was never quite sure how it had happened. One day he was a happy little squirrel racing among the treetops, and the next he was so worried in case he slipped that he got the shivers every time he climbed up to open his door.

Meanwhile, the animals who lived on the ground – the rabbits and mice and the fox family – gathered in a circle to watch and, of course, they had lots of advice to offer, most of which was quite useless. There was such a flapping and twittering; such shaking of the tree and running up and down; so many shouts of "Fetch a rope," and "Get off my wing," and "Do move over and let me try," that Sam woke with a jump and crept timidly outside to see what was causing all the fuss.

For a moment he was unnoticed.

Then a robin saw him and called, "Here's Sam. He'll soon free the Moon – he's stronger than any of us."

Then everyone shouted, "Make way for Sam."

Sam was absolutely terrified. He knew that he could not possibly go right to the end of the swaying branch to help the struggling Moon. At the very thought of it his legs shook and his heart thumped.

On the other hand, to refuse was unthinkable. It would be bad enough to be seen as a coward; it would be worse to leave the Moon wedged in the tree, while creatures needing his light lost their way in the darkness.

Sam was desperate. Suddenly he thought of the Oak Elf, who lived

right beside him. He had seen but never spoken to the Elf, who disliked visitors and was said to be rather cross. But, cross or not, he knew all about magic, and a little magic, Sam felt, was badly needed.

So while the jostling crowd on the oak sorted themselves into order, Sam slipped around the tree to a tiny door hidden behind a spray of ivy, and knocked as loudly as he could.

The door creaked open. Two twinkling brown eyes looked him up and down, and a gruff voice said "Bother the creatures. What is it now? Speak up, squirrel, don't waste my time."

The sharp words startled Sam. But then he saw a great kindness in the Elf's face, and he knew he was not really cross at all. So he took a deep breath and quickly told his story.

"Dear me, what a tangle." The Elf pushed his acorn-cap back off his merry old face and stared thoughtfully at Sam.

"What you need," he said firmly, "is some magic potion."

Looping his long white beard neatly over his arm, he trotted briskly to a cupboard in the room behind him. Taking down a flask, he poured a clear liquid into a tiny crystal goblet which he placed in Sam's shaking paw.

Sam swallowed every drop of the potion. At once his hot dry throat became cool, his cold trembling body grew warm and he felt calm and strong again.

The Elf gave him a little push, and Sam sped outside. Setting his paws on the branch, he scampered along it as swift and sure as ever he had been. Easing the branches aside, he grasped the Moon in one paw and the encircling twigs in the other. Then, while the watchers held their breath, he slowly drew the captive free.

Such a cheer went up as the little Moon soared up into the sky and the light came back to the earth.

Only Sam was quiet. He knew that he could not accept praise that he had not earned, so now he must tell his friends that it was not he, but the Elf, who had saved the Moon. But first, there was something even more important to be done.

He ran back to the Oak Elf, and was in the middle of thanking him for the potion when a very strange thing happened.

"Eh?" The Elf stared at him. "What's that? What potion?"

Sam was amazed. Surely the Elf could not have forgotten so soon.

"The potion you gave me a few minutes ago," he said.

The Elf smiled, then he chuckled and then he roared with laughter.

"There was no potion," he gasped, wiping his eyes with his beard. "I haven't any at the moment. That was spring water you drank."

Then he caught Sam's paw.

"Don't you see? You didn't need any magic. You weren't really afraid – you only thought you were. I knew that when I saw you. Now you have overcome your fear all by yourself – and it will never trouble you again."

And then everyone was crowding around Sam, patting his back and saying "Well done" and pleasant things like that.

And, to the great joy of Sam and his new friend, the wise Elf, it never did.

The Lazy Milkman

It was still dark when *Ting-a-ling-a-ling-a-ling-a-ling* screeched the alarm clock in the tiny bedroom of Rabbits' Rest Cottage.

Joe Rabbit turned over with a snort, twitched his whiskers violently, and pulled the bedclothes over his long brown ears, to shut out the sound.

"Come on, Joe," urged Mrs. Joe, beside him, giving his tail a tweak. "It's half past four. Time to get up."

"Too cold," grunted Joe Rabbit, sleepily. And before you could say "Crisp crunchy cabbages" he was fast asleep and snoring.

"Oh well," grumbled Mrs. Joe to herself, "I'm just going to leave him to sleep for once. That will teach him a lesson. I'm tired of having to nag at him every morning. I guess folks'll just have to wait for their milk for once." So she, too, turned over and settled back to sleep.

Down in the cottage by the holly tree, Bill Hedgehog the Postman was just getting up. He sniffed the frosty air, and a shiver ran through his prickles as he pulled off his red and white striped pyjamas.

Mrs. Hedgehog stirred, and blinked her eyes sleepily.

"Jack Frost's been up to his tricks in the night," grumbled Bill, "and he's frosted the garden like a birthday cake. You just stay tucked up warm, my love, and I'll bring you up a nice, hot cup of tea. Nothing like a good cup of tea to warm up with."

So, hitching up his braces over his prickles, he groped his way down the narrow stairs to the neat little kitchen. There he filled the kettle, and set to work, polishing his boots, while he waited for it to boil. He was

146

always very proud of his shiny boots, and he would not dream of starting his round till he had spent a good ten minutes polishing them.

As soon as the kettle boiled he brewed the tea and set two blue and white mugs on a tray, with a big bowl of sugar. The milk jug was empty, so he stumped across the kitchen to the back door, which he opened a tiny crack, just enough to poke his paw through and reach the icy milk bottle.

Then he stared in surprise, opened the door wider, and gazed at the doorstep. His breath hung in the cold air like smoke, as he stood looking at the empty milk bottle that he had put out the night before.

"What's this?" he muttered angrily to himself. "No milk, and here it is a quarter to seven! where's that Milkman Rabbit, the lazy rascal? Snoring his whiskers off down at Rabbits' Rest, I'll be bound! Well, I guess folks'll just have to wait for their letters for once, for I'm not going out on a frosty morning like this without a drop of hot tea inside me, not for anyone. I reckon I may as well go back to bed for a bit."

So off he went again, up the narrow stairs, grumbling to himself about what he would say to that Joe Rabbit when he saw him.

Meanwhile, down in his tunnel by the big oak tree, Jock Badger, the garage man, had just finished his

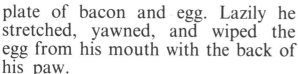

plate of bacon and egg. Lazily he stretched, yawned, and wiped the egg from his mouth with the back of his paw.

"You'd better hurry up," urged Mrs. Badger, who was busy spooning egg into Baby Badger's mouth, as he banged his paws on the tray of his high chair. "It's nearly eight o'clock. You'll be late."

"Can't help that, my dear," grunted Jock, as he settled down to read the *Woodland News*. "I'm waiting for Postman Hedgehog. He's jolly late this morning, and I'm not going out till he's been. You know it's my morning for a letter from Brock."

Brock Badger and Jock Badger were twins, and Brock always wrote to Jock on Mondays and Thursdays, and Jock always wrote to Brock on Tuesdays and Fridays.

"I guess the folks that want petrol will just have to wait for once," he added, turning over the pages of his newspaper.

Down at the coalyard Sam Squirrel, the coalman, had just finished loading his lorry. It was heavy work, heaving up all those sacks on his shoulders, and already his face had several dirty streaks across it, and his fine bushy tail looked like a hearth brush.

"I'll just have to stop at the garage for some petrol," he said as his mate, Micky Mole, climbed up beside him.

The engine started up with a splutter, and the lorry swung away out of the yard. The garage was at the bottom of Mushroom Mound, and Sam pulled up carefully beside the petrol pumps. They waited for a few minutes, but no one came to attend to them, so Sam gave a smart *honk-honk* on the horn. Still no one came, so he climbed out to have a look.

"Well, that's a rum show," he remarked to Mick, pushing back his cap to scratch his head. "Quarter past eight, and no one at the garage. Oh well, I guess folks'll just have to wait for their coal for once. We've got to go to Mr. Owl's house at the top of Acorn Hill, and I can't risk running out of petrol right up there."

At the top of Acorn Hill, Mr. Owl was peering anxiously through the window. It was half-past eight, and he ought to be opening his clean, shining little butcher's shop down in Woodland Way. He couldn't go yet though, because Mrs. Owl had gone to the market at Foxglove Lane, and she had told him before she left to be sure to wait till the coal came, and check that it was put properly in the coal shed. Last time there had been a careless young fellow who had spilt half of it down the garden path, and she didn't want a mess like that to clear up again.

"Oh, well," sighed Mr. Owl, as he polished his glasses gloomily, "I guess folks'll just have to wait for their meat for once." And he picked up the toy mouse that he was carving with his penknife for young Owlet's birthday.

Back at Joe Rabbit's house, Mrs. Joe had not been lazy. Leaving Joe snoring upstairs, she had been up for a long time, cooking breakfast for the six little rabbits. All the five big ones had gone to school, so, as the clock struck nine, she popped Baby Bertie in his pram, and set off for the butcher's shop.

"I'll just have time to get the meat for dinner," she said to herself, "and then I'll be back when the coalman comes, for I don't want to miss him.

There's not a shovelful left in the shed." But, of course, when Mrs. Joe arrived at the butcher's, Mr. Owl was not there.

It must have been about twelve o'clock when the snoring at last stopped, and with a big heave, Joe Rabbit sat up in bed. He stared around him at the daylight, puzzling what day of the week it was. Surely it wasn't his day off . . . was it? He looked at the clock, picked it up, shook it, and held it to his long, floppy ear.

"Well, quiver my whiskers! Here's a fine how-d'you-do!" he exclaimed, springing out of bed. With two long leaps he was down the stairs, and into the kitchen, where Mrs. Joe was ironing his best Sunday shirt.

"Do you know what the time is?" he shouted. "What do you mean by leaving me to sleep like this? Why it's dinnertime. You'd better give me my dinner quick, and then I'll have to rush down to the dairy and start my round."

"Dinner, indeed!" replied Mrs. Joe,

stiffening her ears angrily. "You'd better get yourself a carrot from the garden, for that's all there is to have. I went to the butcher's at nine o'clock, but Mr. Owl hadn't even unlocked his shop."

"Good gracious, that lazy Owl," began Joe Rabbit, but then he stopped, catching sight of the broad grin on his wife's face. "Er – it's jolly cold today," he went on, anxious to change the subject. "Why, the fire's out."

"And well it may be," replied Mrs. Joe, "for not a scrap of coal is there left, and the coalman's not been. I saw his lorry waiting at the garage, but Mr. Badger wasn't there to serve him any petrol."

"Why, whatever's happened to everyone?" asked Joe, scratching his head in bewilderment.

"Well, young Bill Badger was coming along the road, and he said his Dad was sitting at home, waiting for Postman Hedgehog. He said his Dad wasn't going to work until he'd had his letter from his twin brother Brock."

"Postman Hedgehog?" enquired Joe. "By the way, did he bring that packet of lettuce seeds I ordered? They should have come today."

"Lettuce seeds, indeed," snorted Mrs. Joe. "You'll get no lettuce seeds till you get yourself out of bed on time in the morning, Joe Rabbit. I met Mrs. Postman Hedgehog when I was out, and she was grumbling because the milk hadn't come. She said her Bill wasn't starting out on a morning like this without a hot cup of tea, not for anyone."

"You mean he wasn't going to start work till I started work?" asked Joe Rabbit nervously.

"That's just about it," answered Mrs. Rabbit sharply. "You just see what a lot of trouble your laziness has made for people. Bill Hedgehog wouldn't deliver any letters till he'd had a cup of tea, and Jock Badger wouldn't open the garage till he'd got his letter from Brock. Sam Squirrel couldn't deliver the coal till he'd filled up with petrol. Mr. Owl couldn't open his shop till the coal came, and that's why there's nothing in the house for your dinner. So, you see –"

But Joe Rabbit didn't wait to see or hear any more. Mrs. Joe heard the back gate slam, and she looked up just in time to see the flash of Joe's white tail as he raced down the road to the dairy.

And, do you know, he had certainly learnt his lesson, for from that day to this, Joe has never been late again – in fact he is out of bed even before the alarm clock has stopped ringing!

AN ADVENTURE WITH THE WIND

The wind was in a playful mood. He whistled shrilly as he chased the clouds across the sky, and he swept the leaves into a fantastic dance over the cottage garden.

When Mary's mother had rented the cottage, there had been no mention of a cat. Nevertheless, a fine black cat had greeted them on their arrival, leisurely performing his toilet on the doorstep. He was quite friendly, but after drinking their healths in a basin of milk he had spent the remainder of the night singing to the moon.

To-day the wind seemed to excite him too, for he was cutting wild capers, pouncing among the leaves and frisking around Mary's broom.

Everything was a huge joke to the wind, and he was very pleased with himself. In a sudden gust of merriment he whisked the broom down the garden path, with Mary and the cat still clinging to it, and tumbled them on to a heap of leaves in the lane beyond.

"Now, Grimalkin," she grumbled, next time you fall off the broom I will not come and look for you. You should be more careful." Then, noticing Mary, she introduced herself, "I am Susan Peppercorn," she said.

"Why, I do declare, there's my old Bristler!" she said with a laugh. "I thought I had turned him into an ordinary broom when I left him at the village store, but after a thing has once been magicked, you never can tell how it will turn out. Come here, Bristler."

To Mary's astonishment, the broom gently cantered up to the stranger and rubbed itself against the folds of her scarlet dress, while the cat jumped on to her shoulder and affectionately tickled her left ear with his whiskers.

"We've had some good rides together, haven't we?" said Susan Peppercorn, stroking the broom's long handle. "Now, as you can see," she continued, "I am a witch. For hundreds of years we Midnight folk have capered about on broomsticks. Magic carpets have been used — not without a certain amount of success. Seven league boots too have their day, but they were no use to Susan Peppercorn. An aeroplane for

It was rather frightening, but Mary got up and shook the leaves from her dress and looked round for the cat. The cat, it seemed, had found a friend who was playfully scolding him.

Susan Peppercorn! The prettiest little Dragonfly plane that ever was! She's down the lane, so come and examine her."

The witch's Dragonfly was certainly a beauty. There was just enough room for two small people and possibly a cat, to travel comfortably and get a good view. The tail-like body was rounded and jointed in sections of bright metallic green, striped with gold. On either side, in the front, glowed a large ruby lamp, and the ends of the propeller stretched out, quivering like silver antennae.

Two pairs of iridescent wings were extended from the front of the body, shimmering and trembling as if the machine was alive and could hardly wait for its passengers.

The witch beamed with pride. "I'm getting on in years," she said, "but I don't see why I shouldn't keep up to date and enjoy myself as much by day as by night. It is very difficult for me, because aeroplaning is against the rules of the Midnight Folk, and if they catch me in mine I will get into trouble."

The cat jumped eagerly into the cockpit. "Come along, Mary," laughed the witch, "there

is just time for a little trip before the sun sets."

"I don't think," began Mary timidly.

"Stuff and nonsense," protested the witch. "In you go, and Bristler shall fly beneath us," she said, casting a bridle round the broom and jumping into the Dragonfly after Mary.

The Dragonfly rose gracefully from the ground and skimmed smoothly towards the village, the light shining on its translucent wings and flashing from the propeller. The country spread itself like a map beneath them, and the villagers appeared like distant specks.

It was all so exciting that Mary didn't notice that the sun had disappeared and darkness was gathering.

"Goodness gracious," cried Susan Peppercorn, "the moon is up! The Midnight Folk will be on my track! This is just the sort of night to help them. There is nothing that witches like better than a good strong wind, but my Dragonfly can beat them all."

Suddenly the cat arched his back, his fur standing on end.

"Look!" cried Susan Peppercorn, pointing to the moon. "There are three of them! The Midnight Folk are out! We will have more of them before long. We must try and dodge them."

The Dragonfly raced through the sky, and old Bristler seemed to be enjoying himself as he swept along, with the wind ruffling his bristles.

The witch looked anxious. "Listen," she said, "can you hear anything?" Grimalkin was getting excited too, standing on his hind legs and waving his paw in a sweeping circle.

"BROOMSTICKS!" screamed the witch. "They are coming nearer! They must all have turned out! We will be surrounded if we're not careful. You must get away on Bristler, Mary, and Grimalkin and I will stay in the Dragonfly."

"I think I would rather stay with you," said Mary, who was really very much afraid.

"You must do as I say and hurry off at once," urged the witch. "We will go in opposite directions, and while they are wondering which to follow, we can all escape."

She seized Mary roughly and hoisted her on to the broom. The sound of swishing suddenly grew so loud that it was almost deafening. The air was full of gleaming green eyes and fluttering cloaks, and a host of pointed hats aimed, like spears, in the direction of the Dragonfly.

But Bristler was equal to the

occasion. He gave a wild snort and dived earthwards, with Mary clutching tightly to him.

How the wind howled! But Mary was surprised to find that she was no longer afraid, for suddenly the wind ceased and she found herself in the sunlit cottage garden, sweeping the leaves just as if nothing unusual had happened.

Mother was calling, "Tea is ready, Mary, come along! I wonder you are not blown away in this gale. That last gust shook the cottage so that everything rattled. I don't like this wind! It's uncanny."

A light breeze rippled over the garden, like a quiet chuckle of laughter. Mary propped her broom against a tree and eyed it suspiciously. It looked a very commonplace broom, only a handle and some twigs. And yet?

And the cat?

Puss had disappeared, but no doubt he would come back tonight for his basin of milk. In the meantime he was not above suspicion.

And the wind?

Well, the wind chuckled merrily to himself all through the night, so no doubt he had played a trick on somebody.